story by
MEGURU SETO

art by
TOMOYUKI HINO

character design by
TAKEHANA NOTE

Character Guide

Emma Brightness

Noir's friend since childhood. The daughter of a baron, which is a higher rank than baronet. She treats everyone fairly and possesses a kind heart. She gets into the Hero Academy along with Noir.

Noir Stardia

Third son of a baronet, the lowest rank of nobility. In a hidden dungeon, he encounters the super-duper extremely top-class adventurer Olivia Servant and inherits the three most powerful skills in the world—Get Creative, Bestow, and Editor. After overcoming the difficult hurdle of getting into the Hero Academy, he joins the Odin Adventurers' Guild.

Lola

A beautiful receptionist at Odin. She feels affection for Noir and sees Emma, who is close to him, as her rival.

Olivia Servant

A super-duper extremely top-class adventurer. She is currently shackled with Death Chains in a hidden dungeon. To help Noir survive, she passes precious knowledge to him, since he hasn't been an adventurer for very long.

Maria

Daughter of a duke, the highest rank of nobility. Attends the Hero Academy, just like Noir. She is tormented by a powerful curse that will kill her when she turns sixteen—the Sixteenth Year Death Curse.

Alice Stardia

Noir's younger sister. She has a severe brother complex.

CONTENTS

TWEET
TWEET
TWIT TWIT
BIG BROTHER ...

BLINK
ALICE...
EVERY MORNING, MY SISTER WAKES ME UP TENDERLY.

YOU'RE GOING TO MAKE A SPECTACULAR SHOWING AT THE HERO ACADEMY.
AND I'LL WORK HARD TO GET IN NEXT YEAR, EVEN IF IT MEANS COUGHING UP BLOOD.
....
UHH...

YOU DON'T NEED TO GO *THAT* FAR. I'D PREFER IF YOU DIDN'T COUGH UP BLOOD.
ALICE, MY DEAR, SWEET SISTER.

ALICE?
TAP
THAT'S SOMETHING YOU DO WITH YOUR BOYFRIEND.
BROTHERS AND BOY-FRIENDS CAN BE SIMILAR.

SQUEEEEEEZZZE
I FEEL LIKE IF I LET GO OF YOU NOW, YOU'LL FLY FAR AWAY...
I'M JUST GOING TO SCHOOL!

Chapter 8: Fancy Footwork

EVERY DAY BEGINS WITH HUGS FROM MY SISTER.
IT'S A MEANINGFUL AND IMPORTANT ROUTINE.

BEING NOIR, THIRD SON OF THE STARDIA FAMILY... WELL, NO ONE KNOWS WHO I AM.
AS BARONETS, WE'RE AT THE BOTTOM OF THE LADDER. WE'RE POOR... AND NOBILITY IN NAME ONLY.
RECENTLY, A LIBRARIAN JOB WAS STOLEN FROM ME BY SOMEONE OF HIGHER RANK.

BUT I'M ABLE TO KEEP MY CHIN UP BECAUSE OF THE PEOPLE AROUND ME.
LIKE MY FAMILY, AND A LIFELONG FRIEND.

EMMA... SHALL WE DO IT? OUR MORNING GREETING?
UH-HUH!
COME HERE, NOIR...

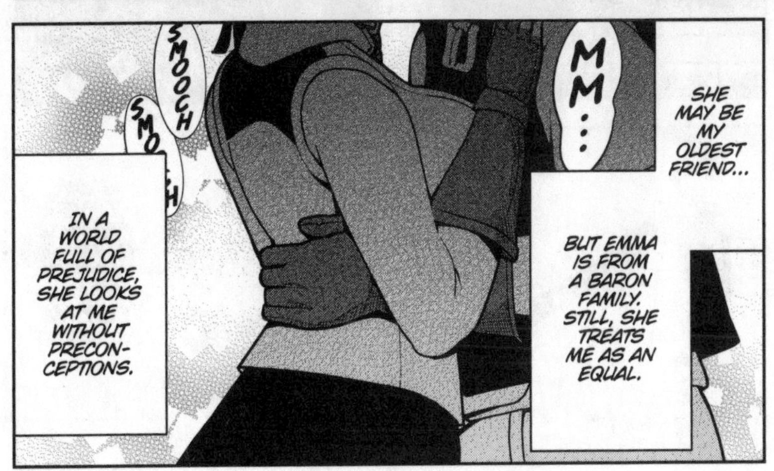
MM...
SMOOCH
SHE MAY BE MY OLDEST FRIEND...
BUT EMMA IS FROM A BARON FAMILY. STILL, SHE TREATS ME AS AN EQUAL.
IN A WORLD FULL OF PREJUDICE, SHE LOOKS AT ME WITHOUT PRECONCEPTIONS.

BUT, UMM... JUST SO NO ONE GETS THE WRONG IDEA...
THIS IS ALSO AN IMPORTANT DAILY ROUTINE.

IT'S NECESSARY TO SPEND LP TO USE MY SKILLS.

GET CREATIVE
Create any skill you can imagine.

EDITOR
Rewrite a skill belonging to you or another person.

BESTOW
Pass a skill you've created on to a person or thing.

THE MORE LP I USE, THE MORE EFFECTIVE THE SKILL. SO THE MORE LP I HAVE, THE BETTER.

I CAN CONVERT FEELINGS OF HAPPINESS OR SATISFACTION INTO LP.

SO I ASK THESE WOMEN TO HELP ME, AND EVERY DAY I SAVE UP.

ドサ
FWUMP
ACK?!
NOIR! A-ARE YOU ALL RIGHT?!
TP
TP
TP

LOLA.

I'M SO SORRY!

THE BOOK'S BAND TORE LOOSE...

ARE YOU HURT, NOIR?

BOMP

I'M FINE. DO YOU HAVE ANY QUESTS YOU CAN RECOMMEND?

I swear... you did that... on purpose...

I DO! ♡ AND WITH YOUR SKILLS, YOU CAN TAKE ON HIGHER-RANK QUESTS RIGHT AWAY!

BESIDES GOING TO THE HERO ACADEMY, I'VE ALSO BECOME AN ADVENTURER.

LOLA IS A GUILD RECEPTIONIST AND A COLLEAGUE I CAN COUNT ON.

THE MORE EXPERIENCED ADVENTURERS AT THE ODIN GUILD HAVE ACCEPTED ME, TOO.

THAT BARBECUE REALLY WAS GREAT...
AHHH!
OH! MISS EMMA! WHAT'S WRONG? YOU'RE SPRAWLED ON THE GROUND.

KEH HEH HEH!

THAT'S NOT A BED DOWN THERE, YOU KNOW...

JOLT

YOU BRAZEN HOME-WRECKER!

I'M VERY PROUD ...
THAT I CAN NOW PASS THROUGH THE GATES OF THE HERO ACADEMY.

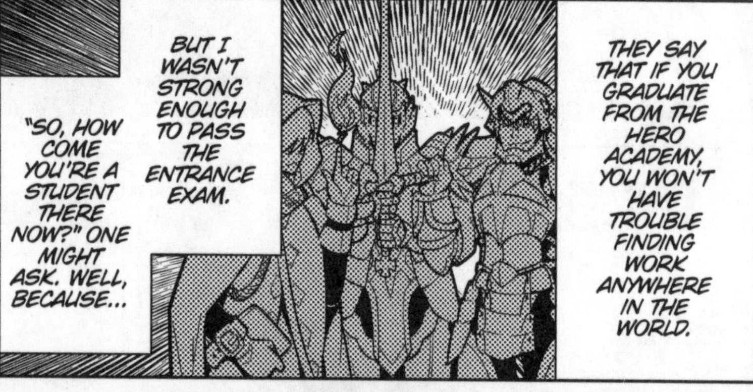
THEY SAY THAT IF YOU GRADUATE FROM THE HERO ACADEMY, YOU WON'T HAVE TROUBLE FINDING WORK ANYWHERE IN THE WORLD.
BUT I WASN'T STRONG ENOUGH TO PASS THE ENTRANCE EXAM.
"SO, HOW COME YOU'RE A STUDENT THERE NOW?" ONE MIGHT ASK. WELL, BECAUSE...

I TRAINED IN SECRET.
AT A HIDDEN DUNGEON ONLY I CAN ENTER.

AND WHAT WAS WAITING FOR ME...

IN THE HIDDEN DUNGEON?

THE SUPER-DUPER EXTREMELY TOP-CLASS ADVENTURER OLIVIA SERVANT, WHO'D BEEN A PRISONER THERE FOR TWO HUNDRED YEARS!!

※ Mental Image.

WITH THE THREE POWERFUL SKILLS SHE TRANSFERRED TO ME--GET CREATIVE, BESTOW, AND EDITOR--I WAS ABLE TO DEFEAT A FORMIDABLE ENEMY...
AND WIN ENTRY INTO THE HERO ACADEMY... AT THE TOP-LEVEL S-CLASS TO BOOT.

THE MORE TRAINING I TAKE ON...
THE MORE MY SITUATION IMPROVES.

GRADUATING FROM THE HERO ACADEMY IS NO LONGER JUST A PIPE DREAM.

IT'S AN OBJECTIVE WITHIN MY REACH.

ガチャ

KA-CHAK

MOST S-CLASS STUDENTS ARE THE CHILDREN OF HIGH-RANKING NOBLES OR WEALTHY ELITES. I'M WELL AWARE OF HOW THE WORLD SEES ME.

OH! IT'S A BAR-ONET ...
BLING

ON THE FIRST DAY OF SCHOOL, WE HAVE TO WEAR A BADGE THAT DISPLAYS OUR FAMILY RANK.
THE SCHOOL SAYS STATUS IS IRRELEVANT, BUT THEN... WHY MAKE US WEAR IT?
IT'S LIKE I'M BEING PUNISHED.

SHFF
PLEASED TO MEET YOU!
HUH?

SLAM

I'M BEN, ELDEST SON OF THE ASTER FAMILY. WE'RE CLOSE AIDES TO THE KING. YOU CAN GUESS THE REST. IT'S A PLEASURE.

CHATTER

I'M FROM THE BLOIS FAMILY! WE'RE A FAMILY OF TRADERS... THE FOURTH RICHEST!

WHOA! SHE'S EXACTLY MY TYPE!

SHE'S SO LOVELY ...

CHATTER

I'M FROM THE BOYLE FAMILY. I CAN PROMISE THE LADY I MARRY A LIFE BUR-DENED BY NOTHING HEAVIER THAN A FEATHER.

CHATTER

NOIR! ARE YOU ALL RIGHT?!

CHATTER

I AM MOST PLEASED TO MAKE YOUR ACQUAINT-ANCE.
SMOOCH
UHH... YES, PLEASED TO MEET YOU, TOO...

EMMA HAS HER LOOKS, AND THAT EASY-TO-GET-ALONG-WITH AURA.
BOYS HAVE BEEN CROWDING AROUND HER SINCE FOREVER.
I'VE ALWAYS BEEN OUTSIDE THE CIRCLE.

WHAT'S THE MATTER? HERE, TAKE MY HAND.
HUH ...?
WELL, THIS IS A SURPRISE! ONE OF THESE BOYS IS ACTUALLY ADDRESSING ME!
NICE TO MEET YOU. I'M FROM THE SIPHONIOUS FAMILY. THE NAME'S--

WHAT THE...?
BLING

OOPS. MY GLASSES WERE CLOUDED UP THERE.
SWFF
WHEW! SURE IS HOT TODAY.
SO, HE HADN'T SEEN MY BADGE.

BARONETS ARE COMMONERS WHO'VE BEEN GIVEN SPECIAL DISPENSATION TO ENTER THE RANKS OF NOBILITY AS A REWARD FOR THEIR SERVICES TO THE COUNTRY.

MOST NOBLES DON'T RECOGNIZE THE EXISTENCE OF BARONETS.

"IT'S A WASTE OF TIME REMEMBERING THE NAMES OF BARONETS."

BUT WHAT DO I CARE? I'M USED TO IT.

UMM... THAT'S QUITE RUDE, ISN'T IT?

CHATTER
ザワ
CHATTER
ザワ
LET ME THROUGH!
OUT OF THE WAY!
CHATTER
ザワ

ザワ...
CHATTER

CLENCH
—

RUDE? ME? WHAT ARE YOU TALKING ABOUT?
NOIR PASSED THE EXAM IN THIRD PLACE!
AND IF HE HADN'T COME BACK WITH THAT DEAD REAPER MATERIAL, *I* WOULDN'T HAVE BEEN ABLE TO PASS AT ALL.

HUH?
HE BRAVED DEATH TO FIGHT IT! SOCIAL STATUS HAS NOTHING TO DO WITH HIS ABILITY TO--
HANG ON A MINUTE. THAT DEAD REAPER WAS THE WORK OF MISS LENORE, FROM AN *EARL* FAMILY.
AAH!

I-INDEED! PLEASE STOP TALKING NONSENSE, MISS EMMA. I BEAT THAT MONSTER BEFORE YOUR VERY EYES.
HEH HEH HEH HEH HEH!
THAT'S RIGHT. WE MADE SURE TO GET OUR STORIES STRAIGHT.

HMPH... TO TELL A LIE WITH THAT PRETTY FACE. I CAN SEE YOU HAVE A TALENT FOR GETTING WHAT YOU WANT.
IN THE END, YOU PASSED THE EXAM WITH "LEFTOVERS," DIDN'T YOU?
......
YOU SAY THINGS LIKE, "I'LL DO WHATEVER IT TAKES!"
AND FLUFF UP THE EGOS OF MEN IN HIGH POSI-TIONS, RIGHT?

OR MAYBE IT'S NOT THEIR *EGOS* YOU'RE FLUFF-ING...
BA HA HA HA HA HA!
AH HA HA HA HA HA!

WHAT TRULY LOVELY WEATHER WE'RE HAVING!
YES, MARIA.

KAICHAK
HUSSSH
OGLE OGLE
OGLE
HM...?
IT'S MARIA!
MARIA ...!
MARIA'S FROM A DUKE FAMILY, THE HIGHEST RANK OF NOBILITY.
SHE'S SO HIGH UP, A BARONET LIKE ME WILL NEVER HAVE ANYTHING TO DO WITH HER.
SPIN
AH!
OH MY!

IT'S AN HONOR TO MEET YOU.
HOW DO YOU DO, NOIR STARDIA?
SHUDDER
......
HUH ...?

WH-WHY WOULD A GREAT LADY LIKE MARIA ...?
SHE'S TALKING TO A TRASH BARONET ...?!

GRIP
BA-DUMP

I LOOK FORWARD TO OUR ACQUAINT-ANCE.
RRRRGH
LIKE-WISE!
MARIA IS EVEN HOLDING HIS HAND ...?!
AND HOW DO YOU DO, EMMA?
H-H-HOW DO YOU DO!

EMMA? SINCE WHEN DO YOU KNOW MARIA?
WHISPER
WHISPER
HUH? THAT'S MY LINE!
HUH?!
I DON'T UNDER-STAND WHAT'S GOING ON...

MARIA... DOESN'T SEEM LIKE A BAD PERSON.
SO THEN WHY...

HAS SHE BEEN STRICKEN WITH A CURSE THAT WILL KILL HER WHEN SHE TURNS SIXTEEN?

LET'S TALK AGAIN SOME-TIME.
EXCUSE US. PLEASE MAKE WAY.

MARIA!
Let Me SAY HeLLO!
SHE REALLY IS POPULAR, ISN'T SHE?

YOU THERE! I MIS-JUDGED YOU. I NEVER WOULD'VE IMAGINED YOU KNOW MARIA!
HAH HAH HAH HAH HAH!
LET'S BE FRIENDS.

ONCE AGAIN...
I'M FROM THE SIPHONIOUS FAMILY. THE NAME IS--
WHAP
NO THANKS.

CRAK
CRAK
YAWWWN...
GULP
BEFORE BECOMING A TEACHER, I WAS A MERCENARY.
FROM THE AGE OF SEVEN TO TWENTY-FOUR.
TUP

MY NAME IS ELENA STONGS.

THIS PERSON'S A TEACHER?!
OUTSIDE THE CAPITAL, IT'S MONSTERS AND BANDITS EVERYWHERE.
IF YOU'RE NOT CAREFUL, YOU'LL BE KILLED IN A SINGLE BLOW.

SO TODAY WE'RE GOING TO PRACTICE DEFENSE.
NOW THEN... NOIR STARDIA, STEP FORWARD.
CHFF
BA-DUMP
BA-DUMP
THP

ATTACK ME WITH YOUR SWORD...
AND WITH INTENT TO KILL.
MMFF!
HUH? BUT WHAT IF--
RELAX. YOU WON'T EVEN SCRATCH ME.
HMPH...!
WHY IS SHE SO SURE OF HERSELF?
TIME TO USE DIS-CERNING EYE!

I'M AT LEVEL 35.

Lv.232

Name: Elena Stongs
Age: 24
Race: Human
Level: 232
Class: Schoolteacher
Skills: Stamina Up, Martial Arts (Grade A), Earthen Wall, Earthen Bullet, Heal

J-JUST WHAT YOU'D EXPECT FROM A FORMER MERCENARY...

IT WOULD BE RUDE NOT TO GIVE IT ALL I'VE GOT!
THTT
BODY AND SOUL!

SWING THROUGH COMPL--

CHSSSSK
WHOOMF

SHFF
WHSSSH

THE BACK-STEP.
YOU'RE GOING TO LEARN HOW TO DO IT RIGHT NOW.

......
ALL RIGHT. WE'LL TAKE TURNS ON OFFENSE AND DEFENSE. MIMIC WHAT I DID BEFORE.
JUST DRAW THE ATTACKER'S ATTENTION, THEN LEAP BACKWARD. EASY, RIGHT?
HERE I COME!

CRAK
KRUNCH
KRAK
CRUK

NOIR!!

NOW WE CAN HAVE SOME MORE FUN! ♡

TREMBLE TREMBLE

MARIA?!

SHE'S NOT A TOUGH TEACHER, SHE'S JUST *TOUGH*...

HE'LL BE ALL RIGHT. I'LL USE MY HEALING MAGIC.

OH, AND AN-OTHER THING. IF YOU DO A SUCCESSFUL BACKSTEP, I'LL GIVE YOU A SPECIAL REWARD.

A REWARD?

Got healed.

IF ANY OF THE BOYS EVADE EVEN ONE OF MY ATTACKS...
I'LL DO SOMETHING NICE FOR THEM.
OAAHH
WHOOO

NOIR STARDIA, YOU BETTER SCREW UP!
I'M GOING TO GET THE TEACHER'S REWARD!
BOYS ARE SO...
GOOD GRIEF.

IF I BACKSTEP AND DODGE HER WOODEN PRACTICE SWORD, I WIN.
WHOMF
WHOMF
I DON'T WANT TO GET HURT AGAIN...
RIGHT! I'LL USE GET CREATIVE TO TAKE HER ON.

Current LP: 2200
TOO EXPENSIVE!
HMM... WELL, HOW ABOUT THIS?!
MARTIAL ARTS C
LP Cost: 1000
LP Left: 1200

IMPROVED BACKSTEP
NOW THAT'S A GOOD COST-PERFORMANCE RATIO!
I'LL SPEND THE LP AND GET THE SKILL!
LP Cost: 200
LP Left: 2000

UH!

NO! WA--

DON'T! LOSE!
WHUMF
FOCUS!!

CHSSSSK

WHSSSSH
SHFF
......

IF I'M ABLE TO DODGE WITH A BACK-STEP...
THEN I GET IT, RIGHT?

SHALL I ACCEPT MY REWARD?

UHH...

THE REWARD YOU PROMISED, MISS ELENA?

Chapter 8 / End

◆BIG BROTHER ANTENNA◆

BEEP BEEP

CLATTER

"REWARD" ...? "TEACHER" ...? ANOTHER NEW WOMAN ?!

OUT OF THE WAY, BIG BROTHER, OR I CAN'T KILL HER!

HUSSSH
GOOD MORNING, ALICE.

HRMF!
SIR, ARE YOU OKAY WITH THIS?
LEAVE HER BE.
SHE'LL GET FIRST PLACE ON THE NEXT EXAM.
ALICE STARDIA IS A UNIQUE GIRL.

THE
HIDDEN
DUNGEON
ONLY I CAN
ENTER

MISS ELENA.

SHE TRAINED AS A MERCENARY FROM CHILDHOOD.

AND THAT TOUGHNESS ISN'T JUST IN HER BODY. IT'S IN HER MIND, TOO.

SHE'S AN ADULT WOMAN WHO'S ALWAYS COOL AND COLLECTED.

AND THE REWARD FROM SUCH A WOMAN...

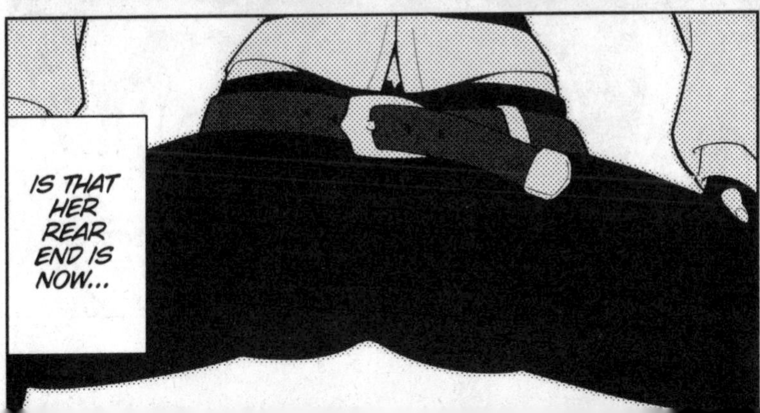

Chapter 9: Breakfall

URGH!
GAH!
AWW... I CAN'T BELIEVE HE'S THE ONLY ONE WHO PASSED THE BACKSTEP LESSON!

AIEEE!
HEY! THIS IS YOUR PRECIOUS REWARD!
THAT'S RIGHT! YOU OUGHTA BE MOANING HAPPILY!
IDIOTS.

REWARD? IS THIS A JOKE? THIS IS AGONIZING! AND EMBAR-RASSING!
WHAP
AUGH!
UNGH...!
WHAP

SQUISH
I THOUGHT EMMA WAS THE ONE PERSON WHO ALWAYS HAD MY BACK...
MISS ELENA, PLEASE STOP! I'M ALREADY DEAD!

ALL RIGHT! REWARD AND BREAK TIME IS OVER!

WAS IT SOFT? WHAT DID IT SMELL LIKE?

TEACHER'S BUTT!

DUDE, I'M SO JEALOUS! I WISH SHE WOULD DO ME, TOO!

BOP

MMMF!

YOU THERE. SHUT UP.

NOW, FORM PAIRS.

BLUR
BLUR
NOIR, YOU AREN'T ADDICTED NOW, ARE YOU? TO HER BEHIND?
OF COURSE NOT! I'VE HAD MY FILL!
THANK GOOD-NESS! LET'S PAIR UP, THEN! ♪

I'D LIKE HER TO DO THAT BUTT GRIND AGAIN.
I GAINED 400 LP FROM THAT!
DEEP DOWN, AM I A MASO-CHIST?

YOU TWO.
I WANT YOU TO FIND OTHER PART-NERS.
HUH?
ROMANTIC COUPLES CONSPIRE TOGETHER.
WE'RE NOT A ROMANTIC COUPLE.

REALLY ...?
NOPE, NOT YET.

ANYWAY, I WON'T ALLOW YOU TO PAIR UP.
SOMEONE ELSE PLEASE PARTNER WITH NOIR!

SWSH

YOU DO IT. YOU SPOKE TO HIM BEFORE, DIDN'T YOU?
NAW, I WAS ONLY INTER-ESTED IN MISS ELENA'S BUTT.
I'LL PARTNER WITH EMMA, SO YOU GO WITH HIM.
HUH?! YOU TRYING TO FOIST A BARONET LOSER ONTO ME?!

IN THAT CASE, PLEASE JOIN HANDS WITH ME, MARIA.

SWISH

......

WHUP

I WASN'T SPEAKING TO *YOU*, ATTENDANT WOMAN.

WE'RE FELLOW DUKES.
THOSE IN LOFTY POSITIONS SHOULD WORK TOGETHER FOR MUTUAL BENEFIT.
GRIP

SHWFF
I MUST DE-CLINE.

......
CHFF
EVERY-ONE... PLEASE LISTEN.

BEING BORN INTO A DUCAL FAMILY WAS SHEER LUCK.
CHFF
EVERY DAY, I STRIVE TO BE WORTHY OF THAT NOBLE RANK.

CHFF
I RE-SPECT...
PEOPLE BORN INTO BARONET FAMILIES.
THE REASON BEING...
THAT THEY WERE WARRIORS WHO DEDICATED THEIR LIVES TO THIS COUNTRY. THEY ARE FAR MORE DIGNIFIED THAN THE RANK BESTOWED UPON THEM.

CHFF

A BARONET IS MORE EARNEST AND FAITH-FUL THAN A FAMILY OF HIGH STANDING...
WHICH DOES NO MORE THAN BRANDISH ITS NOBLE STATUS.
AND THAT'S WHO I'D LIKE TO BE WITH.

HUSSSH
NOD
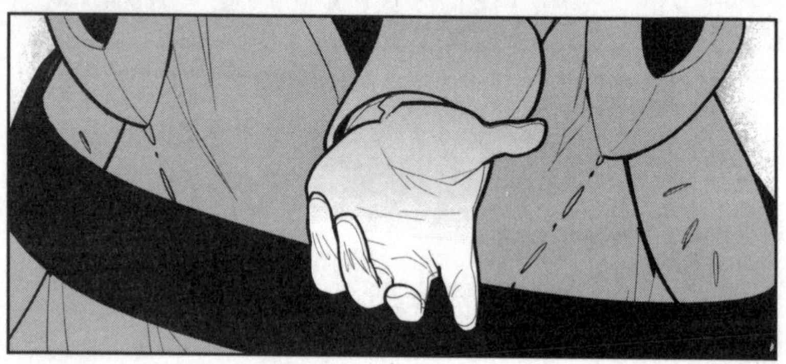

NOIR.

WOULD YOU PLEASE JOIN HANDS WITH ME?

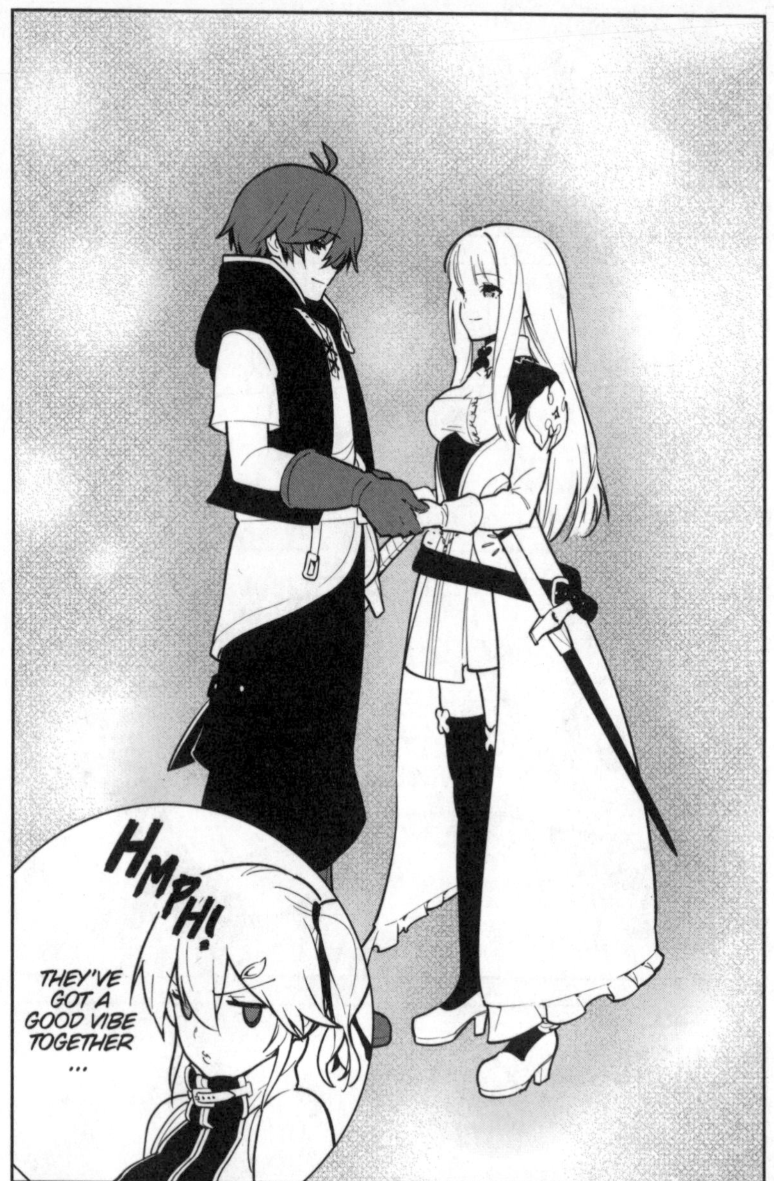
HMPH!
THEY'VE GOT A GOOD VIBE TOGETHER ...

NEXT, WE'LL BE PRACTICING BREAK-FALLS.
DO SEVERAL THROWS AND AL-TERNATE.

MARIA!! IS SOME-THING WRONG?!
IT'S JUST, NOW THAT I'M FREE OF THAT TENSION, I SUD-DENLY FEEL...

SO, SHE HAD TO MUSTER HER COURAGE TO MAKE THAT SPEECH.
I'M... REALLY GRATE-FUL FOR WHAT YOU SAID.
YOU'RE WELCOME.

NOIR...
AAH...
MARIA...

BREAKFALL
LP Cost: 30

NO QUESTION, I'LL TAKE THAT!

IS IT CHEAP BECAUSE I HAVE AN AFFINITY FOR IT?

MY WHOLE LIFE HAS BEEN ONE BIG BREAKFALL. SHEESH.

WHAM

YES! IT WORKED!

AWGH?!

SQUISH

NOIR STARDIA!
A-AMANE!
GULP
TRUD TRUD TRUD TRUD TRUD
AIEEE!
MMNF MMNF MMNF!
(I'VE BEEN FALSELY ACCUSED!)

DON'T MOVE, STARDIA.

MARIA!!

YOU MUSTN'T PUSH YOURSELF SO HARD.
I'M FINE. I JUST FEEL A TINY PAIN IN MY CHEST...
MURMUR
MURMUR
YOU'RE LYING. LOOK HOW MUCH YOU'RE SWEATING. YOU NEED REST.

TICK

OH!
OF COURSE. THIS IS...

THE SIX-TEENTH YEAR DEATH CURSE.
"THAT GIRL HAS BEEN CURSED.
"SHE'S GOING TO DIE. ON HER SIX-TEENTH BIRTH-DAY."
IT'S A FIT CAUSED BY THE CURSE.

I'LL COME TO CHECK ON HER ONCE THE LESSON IS OVER.

MAYBE I SHOULD TRY...
MY EDITOR SKILL!

SIXTEENTH YEAR DEATH CURSE

Causes acute pain through the entire body on a fixed cycle.

When the afflicted turns sixteen, they die.

Erase with Editor

LP Cost: 8000

TOO EXPENSIVE. THAT'S A SERIOUSLY POWERFUL CURSE.

ISN'T THERE ANYTHING I CAN DO?
ANSWER ME, GREAT SAGE.

WHEN IS HER BIRTHDAY?
THE ANSWER... IS JUNE 6.
!!
BUT THAT'S...

ONE WEEK FROM NOW, MARIA WILL LOSE HER LIFE TO THE CURSE.

THERE'S NO TIME LEFT.
WHAT IS THE MOST EFFECTIVE MEANS FOR ME TO AMASS LP RIGHT NOW?

THE ANSWER... IS THAT THERE IS A WAY TO ACQUIRE 2000 LP.
OOH!

PUT ALL OF THE WOMEN HERE IN A LINE.
HM? OKAY, OKAY!

NEXT, TOUCH EACH OF THEIR BOSOMS.
HUHHH...?

IF YOU ARE SUCCESSFUL WITH ALL OF THEM--
I CAN'T DO THAT! ALSO, I'VE GOT A BLINDING HEAD-ACHE!!
THIS BAD, EVEN WITH MY HEADACHE IMMUNITY?!

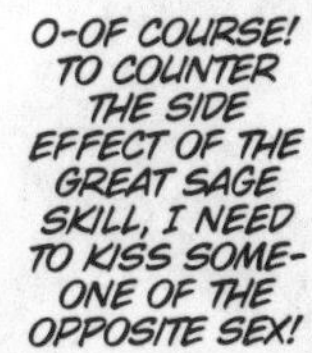
O-OF COURSE! TO COUNTER THE SIDE EFFECT OF THE GREAT SAGE SKILL, I NEED TO KISS SOME-ONE OF THE OPPOSITE SEX!

GRIP
ガッ
HUH? NOIR, YOU DON'T LOOK WELL.
GIVE ME... GIVE ME TODAY'S GREETING, PLEASE!

HERE?! BUT THERE ARE PEOPLE AROUND!
I CAN'T TAKE IT! I'M SO SORRY!
がばっ
GRAB

?!
むち
SMOO..
ゆ〜
OOCH ♥

MISS ELENA.
SHE TRAINED AS A MERCE-NARY FROM CHILD-HOOD.
AND THAT TOUGHNESS ISN'T JUST IN HER BODY. IT'S IN HER MIND, TOO.

SHE'S AN ADULT WOMAN WHO'S ALWAYS COOL AND COLLECTED.

FIFTEEN LAPS AROUND THE SCHOOLYARD! SPRINTING! AT FULL SPEED!!

YES, MA'-AAAM!

Odin Adventurers' Guild

HELLO, LOLA.
JOLT
HUH?! NOIR?! WHY ARE YOU HERE NOW?!

DASH
HUH? LOLA?
Y-YOU SHOULD HAVE WARNED ME YOU WERE COMING!
PLEASE GIVE ME TEN-- NO, FIVE MINUTES!

WHAT WAS THAT ABOUT?
SHE'S FIXING HER MAKEUP.
SEEMS SHE CUT SOME CORNERS WITH IT TODAY BECAUSE SHE THOUGHT YOU WEREN'T COMING.
RUSTLE RUSTLE
NOW THAT I THINK ABOUT IT, THERE WAS SOME-THING DIFFER-ENT ABOUT HER.

BUT LOLA WOULD LOOK FINE WITHOUT ANY MAKE-UP.
NOIR, FORGET ABOUT THAT PAINTED WOMAN.
I CAN'T DO THAT. LOLA IS THE RECEP-TIONIST WHO HANDLES ME.
HMPH! IDIOT!

AND WHAT I NEED NOW...
I CAN ONLY TURN TO LOLA FOR.

A SIX-
TEENTH
YEAR
DEATH
CURSE,
YOU
SAY...?
CLACK

THAT'S A POWERFUL CURSE-CATEGORY SKILL.

YES. OUR FRIEND IS IN TROUBLE...

AND WE'RE LOOKING FOR A WAY TO LIFT THE CURSE.

THE ODIN GUILD IS AN ASSOCIATION FOR ADVENTURERS THAT HAS EXISTED FOR OVER TWO HUNDRED YEARS.

MY MASTER, OLIVIA, WAS ALSO A REGISTERED MEMBER.

A GUILD RECEPTIONIST WHO'S KNOWLEDGEABLE ABOUT SKILLS...

SHOULD KNOW HOW TO GET RID OF MARIA'S CURSE.

HUH?! SUCH A SICKNESS... IT CAN'T BE! ESPECIALLY ON A DUKE'S DAUGHTER...

CLACK

WE TEND TO THINK THAT NOBILITY WANT FOR NOTHING.

YES. THEY DON'T SHOW IT ON THE SURFACE...

BUT THEY MUST STRUGGLE LIKE US SOMETIMES.

HER FINAL DAY IS JUNE 6.
ONE MORE WEEK TILL MARIA DIES.
22 23 24 25 26
29 30 31
5 6
NEED 8000LP
I NEED 8000 LP TO GET RID OF THE CURSE WITH EDITOR.
THAT'S NOT AN AMOUNT... I CAN ACQUIRE IN A WEEK.

I KNOW IT'S BEYOND ME, BUT...
"A BARONET IS MORE EARNEST AND FAITHFUL THAN A FAMILY OF HIGH STANDING...
"WHICH DOES NO MORE THAN BRANDISH ITS NOBLE STATUS.
"AND THAT'S WHO I'D LIKE TO BE WITH."
I WISH I COULD BE OF SOME HELP TO MARIA.

I BELIEVE THERE'S A WAY TO NEUTRALIZE THE CURSE.
IF YOU WERE A CLERIC, WHO EXORCISES EVIL...
CLERIC?

LUNA HEELA.
SHE'S A FRIEND OF MINE.
CAN WE DEPEND ON HER?

THAT'S THE THING. SHE'S IN HIGH DEMAND AND ALWAYS BUSY.
SHE'S BOOKED TO SEE PATIENTS THREE MONTHS IN ADVANCE.
NOIR! SHE COULD BE...
YEAH, SOUNDS HOPE-FUL.

BUT... IT'LL PROBABLY BE DIFFICULT.
SHE ALMOST NEVER LIFTS CURSE-CATEGORY SKILLS.
HMMMooo
WHY NOT ...?!

SHE INSISTS THAT IT'S NOT A MATTER OF MONEY.
IT'S TERRIBLE. I'M HER FRIEND, AND SHE WON'T EVEN TELL *ME* WHY.
......
SHOULD WE DROP THE IDEA?
OF COURSE NOT!
PLEASE INTRODUCE US. WE HAVE TO AT LEAST TALK WITH HER.

SO... SHE'S RELUCTANT TO LIFT CURSE-CATEGORY SKILLS.
COULD IT BE THAT WHEN SHE DOES...
SHE LOSES SOMETHING MORE IMPORTANT THAN MONEY?

IF I DON'T DO IT...

CLENCH

THEN WHO WILL?

"WOULD YOU PLEASE JOIN HANDS WITH ME?"

SHE CAME...

TO MY RESCUE...

THEN.

IT'S MY TURN TO RESCUE HER.
SEVEN DAYS UNTIL MARIA DIES.

Chapter 9 / End

◆MISS ELENA'S SHOULDER MASSAGE① ◆

THE
HIDDEN
DUNGEON
ONLY I CAN
ENTER

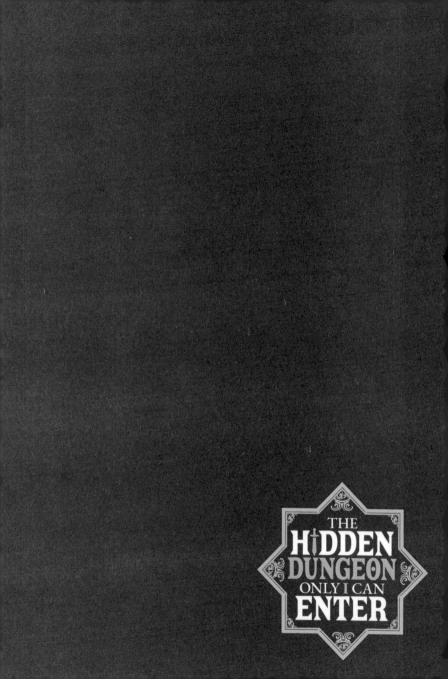

Chapter 10: Luna the Cleric

Temple on the Outskirts of the Royal Capital

SHE'S ALWAYS AT THE TEMPLE ...

THIS TIME OF DAY.

KOFF!
KOFF!
HRRNN...
......
HAH HAH HAH!
HEH HEH HEH HEH!

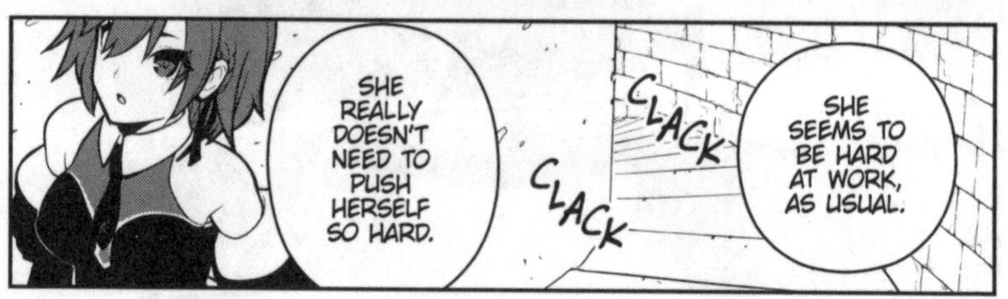

"A SIXTEENTH YEAR DEATH CURSE... THAT'S A POWERFUL CURSE-CATEGORY SKILL."
"YES, AND WE'RE LOOKING FOR A WAY TO LIFT IT."

"LUNA.

"SHE'S A CLERIC WHO EXORCISES EVIL INFLUENCES, SO IT MIGHT BE POSSIBLE.

"SHE'S MY FRIEND, AND HER ABILITY IS AUTHENTIC.

"BUT SHE ALMOST NEVER LIFTS CURSES."

I'M HAVING A SHORT REST. WAIT, PLEASE.

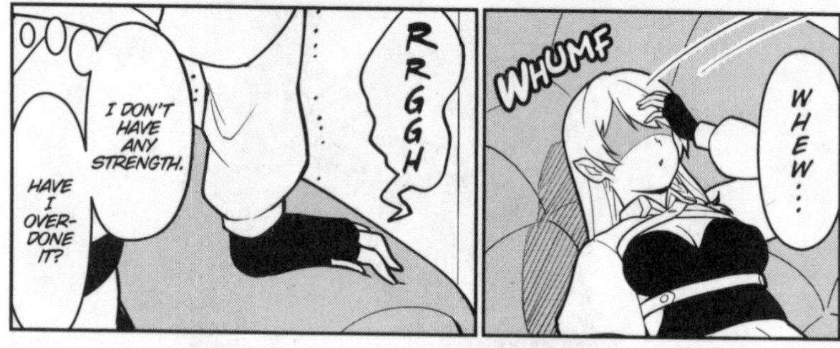
WHUMF
WHEW...
RRGGH
...
I DON'T HAVE ANY STRENGTH.
HAVE I OVERDONE IT?

SLUMP
!
THERE NOW, HOLD ON TO ME, LUNA.

ONCE I COULD RELAX, I WASN'T REALLY PAYING ATTENTION.

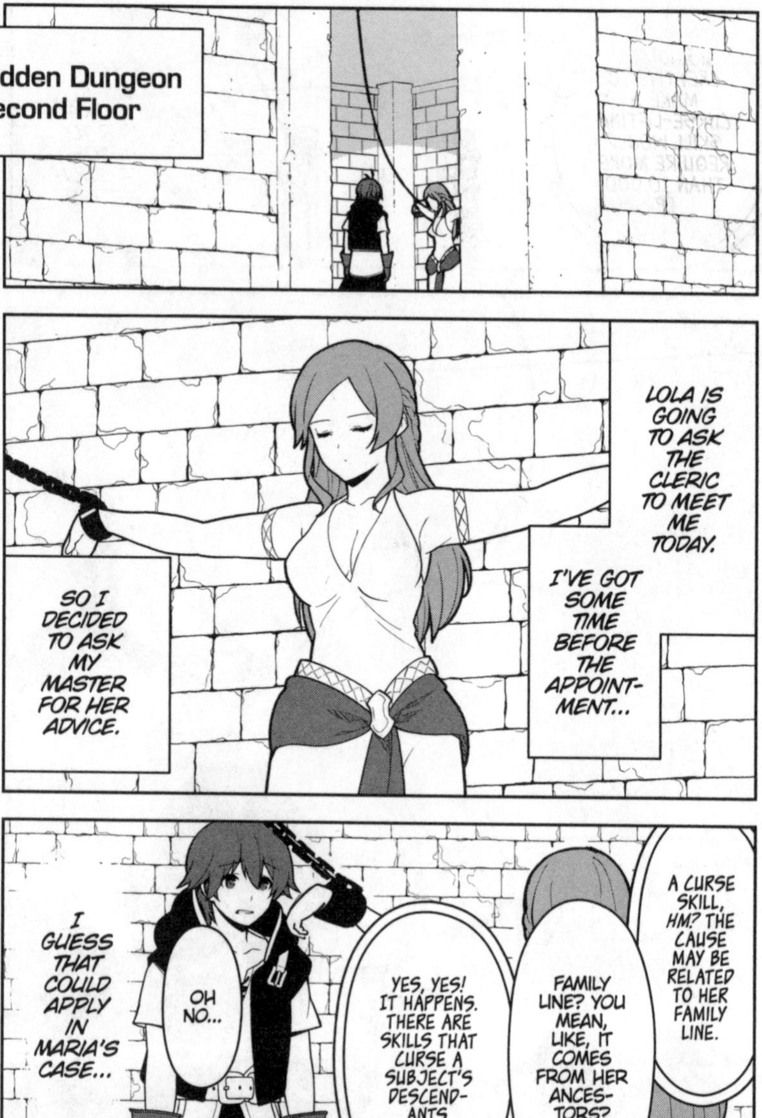

Hidden Dungeon Second Floor

LOLA IS GOING TO ASK THE CLERIC TO MEET ME TODAY.

I'VE GOT SOME TIME BEFORE THE APPOINTMENT...

SO I DECIDED TO ASK MY MASTER FOR HER ADVICE.

A CURSE SKILL, HM? THE CAUSE MAY BE RELATED TO HER FAMILY LINE.
FAMILY LINE? YOU MEAN, LIKE, IT COMES FROM HER ANCESTORS?
YES, YES! IT HAPPENS. THERE ARE SKILLS THAT CURSE A SUBJECT'S DESCENDANTS.
OH NO...
I GUESS THAT COULD APPLY IN MARIA'S CASE...

BUT THAT DOESN'T MAKE IT OKAY FOR HER TO HAVE TO SUFFER SUCH MISFORTUNE.
USING GET CREATIVE TO MAKE A CURSE-LIFTING SKILL WOULD REQUIRE MORE THAN 10,000 LP.
STAY OUT OF IT, AND LEAVE THINGS TO THE CLERIC.
I WONDER WHAT SHE'S LIKE.
IF SHE HAS PURIFICA-TION SKILLS, THEN SHE MUST BE OF ELVEN STOCK.
WOW! AN ELF... YOU ALMOST NEVER SEE THEM.
SHIIIINE
YOU CAN ALSO SATE YOUR LUST WITH OTHER SPECIES!
YOU'LL AMASS A LOT OF LP FROM IT.
SAY WHAT ?!

I'LL... AIM TO DO THAT!

YOU HAVE TO!

OOH!♡

IS THIS FOR REAL?!

BY THE WAY, MASTER, HAVE YOU EVER GOTTEN 8000 LP IN ONE WEEK?

8000 LP? IF YOU FORGET ABOUT ANY RULES, IT CAN BE DONE.

THIS IS WHAT I'D DO.

I'LL SAY IT IN YOUR EAR.

MURMUR

FIRST... I'D INCREASE SENSI-TIVITY OVER MY ENTIRE BODY...

THEN... AND TIE UP... AND... WHILE STILL...

MURMUR

NOW!♪ IF YOU ASK YOUR LIFELONG FRIEND TO DO EVERYTHING I JUST TOLD YOU, IT'LL BE A PIECE OF CAKE, RIGHT?

HOW DO I USE THESE ...?

NO, NO, NO, NEVER, NEVER, NEVER!!

HAH HAH HAH! JUST KIDDING! YOU'RE SO CUTE!♪
QUIT TOYING WITH ME ALREADY ...

ANY-THING ELSE YOU NEED TODAY?
PLEASE TELL ME ABOUT SKILLS I CAN USE TO EARN LP.
OKAY!♪ I, YOUR GREAT MENTOR, OLIVIA, WILL IMPART SOME WISDOM.
YES, MA'AM!

RATATAT
NOW THEN, MY WISDOM CON-CERNS...
WHICH FORBIDDEN SKILL HAS THE BEST COST-PERFOR-MANCE RATIO!
RATATAT
RATATAT
RATATAT

WHAM
WHAAAAHHHH?!
LUCKY LECHER

LUCKY LECHER
Spend 300 LP to acquire!
THE EF-FECTS, WELL...
YOU'LL EXPE-RIENCE THEM SOON ENOUGH!
GULP

WHAT THE...?! IT'S ALREADY TIME FOR THE MEETING.
THAT'LL HAVE TO BE IT FOR TODAY.
HUH?!

COME BACK SOON, ALL RIGHT? IF YOU DON'T, I, OLIVIA, WILL DIE OF LONELI-NESS.
SURE, SURE.
YOU REALLY ARE TROUBLE, YOU KNOW?

WHEN I'M WITH OLIVIA, I LOSE TRACK OF TIME.
SHE'S SO FUN, AND THE OP-PORTUNITY TO LEAVE JUST SLIPS AWAY...
I'LL BE BACK TO SEE YOU AGAIN SOON, MASTER...
WITH GOOD NEWS ABOUT MARIA AS A BONUS.

OH! NOIR! YOU'RE SO LATE!
THE CLERIC MUST ALREADY BE WAITING!
SORRY, SORRY!
MEOW! ♥
STUMBLE
WHOA!

ばいーん
BA-YOING

IN THE FUTURE, I'LL RELATE TODAY'S OCCURRENCE AS...

"THE TIME I FELL INTO AN AMPLE BOSOM."

WHAH?!

WHUSH
FLASH
GYAAH?!
OOH!

IT'S DIFFERENT THAN I IMA-GINED!
THIS SKILL IS INCRED-IBLE!
OLIVIA REALLY IS SOME-THING ELSE!!
300 LP acquired!

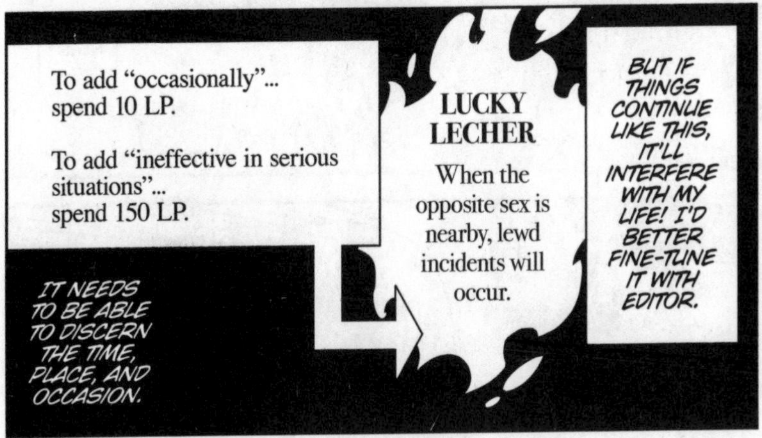
BUT IF THINGS CONTINUE LIKE THIS, IT'LL INTERFERE WITH MY LIFE! I'D BETTER FINE-TUNE IT WITH EDITOR.
LUCKY LECHER
When the opposite sex is nearby, lewd incidents will occur.
To add "occasionally"... spend 10 LP.
To add "ineffective in serious situations"... spend 150 LP.
IT NEEDS TO BE ABLE TO DISCERN THE TIME, PLACE, AND OCCASION.

WAHOO!
LUNA.

HE CERTAINLY SEEMS LIKE A SKIRT-CHASER.
HE'S QUITE DIFFERENT FROM WHAT YOU TOLD ME, LOLA.
YOU THINK SO? YOU THINK NOIR IS A WILD ANIMAL ON THE INSIDE?

NOIR, *EH...?*
HMM...

HE'S GOT A CUTE FACE, DOESN'T HE?

MY TYPE.

WHAH?! LUNA! WHAT ARE YOU TALKING ABOUT?!

CHATTER
CHATTER
OH! NOIR, OVER THERE!

CHATTER
IT'S LOLA, AND...
CHATTER
IS THAT THE CLERIC? SHE REALLY STANDS OUT...
CHATTER

THIS IS THE CLERIC ...
LUNA HEELA. PLEASED TO MEET YOU.
I'VE RESERVED A TABLE FOR US. WE'LL TALK IN HERE.

WHOA... THAT SILKY SILVER HAIR, AND THE LOVELY CURVE OF HER BACK...
THAT FIRM BEHIND, AND THOSE LONG, SLENDER LEGS...
SHE'S SUPER BEAUTI-FUL!!! I SHOULD NEVER HAVE LET NOIR MEET HER!
MY CHEST'S THE ONLY THING BETTER THAN HERS...
BOO-HOO!
HM? COME ON!

CLACK
SO, WE HAVE A REQUEST TO ASK OF YOU.
CLACK
WE'D LIKE YOU TO EXAMINE A FRIEND OF OURS, A WOMAN.
ALL RIGHT. WHAT'S HER NAME?

MARIA. SHE'S THE DAUGHTER OF A DUKE.
HALT

I KNOW ABOUT HER. SHE'S CURSED, ISN'T SHE?
CLACK
I EXAMINED HER ONCE BEFORE, BUT I HAD TO DECLINE HELPING HER.

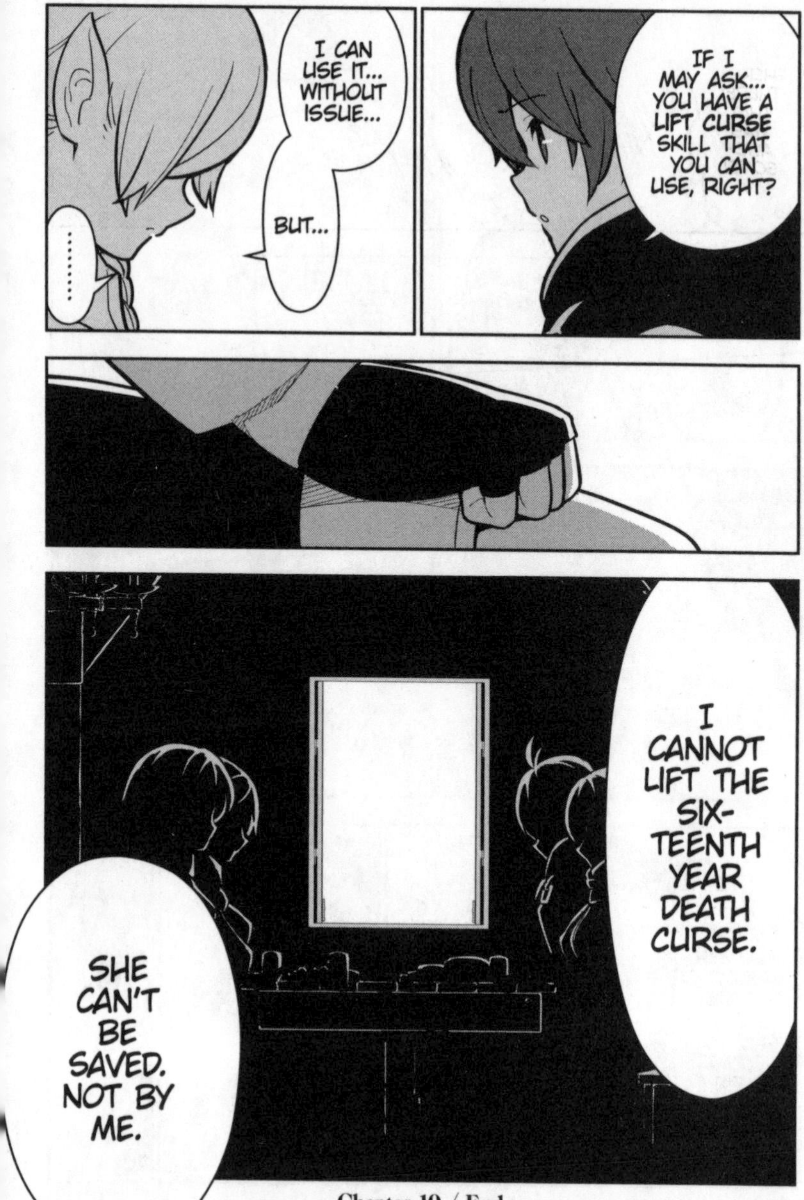

I CANNOT LIFT THE SIX-TEENTH YEAR DEATH CURSE.

SHE CAN'T BE SAVED. NOT BY ME.

Chapter 10 / End

◆MISS ELENA'S SHOULDER MASSAGE②◆

THE
HIDDEN
DUNGEON
ONLY I CAN
ENTER

Chapter 11: Close Friend

I CANNOT LIFT THE SIXTEENTH YEAR DEATH CURSE.

SHE CAN'T BE SAVED. NOT BY ME.

SHE HAS LESS THAN A WEEK TO LIVE.
SHE HAS FITS OF PAIN THROUGH-OUT HER BODY...
AND THE INTERVALS BETWEEN THEM ARE BECOMING SHORTER.

LESS THAN A WEEK?!
SO, HER FINAL DAY DRAWS NEAR...

LUNA, YOU DON'T NEED TO FEEL RESPON-SIBLE FOR THIS.
YOU SAVE DOZENS OF PEOPLE EVERY DAY.
THAT ALONE IS PRAISE-WORTHY.

IT SEEMS LIKE LUNA... FEELS OVERLY RESPONSIBLE?

SHE MUST HAVE SOME SECRET. TIME FOR MY DISCERNING EYE.

Name: Luna Heela
Age: 17
Race: Half Elf
Level: 35
Class: Cleric, Adventurer
Skills: Magical Firearms (Grade B), Energizing Shot, Healing Shot, Fainting Spell, Lift Curse

I'M CURIOUS ABOUT THE LAST TWO. I'LL INVESTIGATE LIFT CURSE FIRST.

LIFT CURSE

Erases curse-category skills. The user's lifespan diminishes based on the strength of the curse.

LUNA PROBABLY CAN LIFT MARIA'S CURSE, BUT IN EXCHANGE, IT WOULD SHAVE OFF A LOT OF HER OWN LIFE.
EXCHANGE
ELVES LIVE MANY TIMES LONGER THAN HUMANS.
PERHAPS THE CURSE ON MARIA IS SO POWERFUL THAT EVEN THE LIFESPAN OF AN ELF COULDN'T COVER IT?

NOIR... PLEASE SHOW ME TO MISS MARIA'S HOUSE.
I WILL RELEASE HER FROM THE CURSE.
ARE YOU SURE, LUNA? I THOUGHT YOU COULDN'T LIFT HER CURSE.
EMMA AND LOLA, COULD YOU PLEASE GIVE US A MINUTE? I'D LIKE TO TALK TO LUNA ALONE.

I SNUCK A PEEK AT YOUR SKILLS WITH MY DISCERNING EYE.
I'M SORRY.
THERE'S A PRICE TO PAY FOR LIFT CURSE, HUH?
IF YOU HEAL MARIA, THEN YOU--

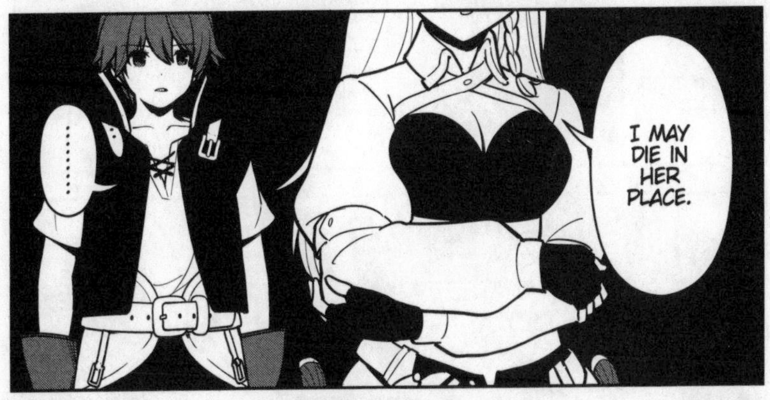
I MAY DIE IN HER PLACE.
......

BUT KNOWING THAT ANOTHER LIFE IS ABOUT TO BE SNUFFED OUT, I CAN'T STAND BY AND DO NOTHING.
I WANT TO SAVE PEOPLE.
LIKE MY MOTHER DID.

MY MOTHER WAS A CLERIC WHO HAD THE LIFT CURSE SKILL, JUST LIKE ME.
SHE KEPT ON USING IT, EVEN THOUGH SHE KNEW FULL WELL IT WAS SHORTEN-ING HER TIME HERE.
SHE GAVE HER LIFE FOR THE CHILDREN OF COMPLETE STRANGERS.
AND NOW SHE'S GONE FROM THIS WORLD.

I HAVE INHERITED THE BLOOD OF MY MOTHER, AND SO--
CRUMBL CRUMBL
ドガ
KA-DOOM
?!

THERE'S A CHILD TRAPPED UNDER HERE! SOMEBODY HELP!
IS THERE ANYONE HERE WHO CAN USE RECOVERY MAGIC?!

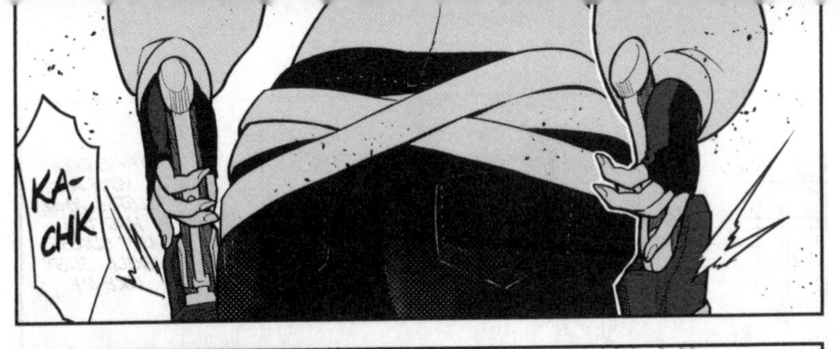

FWIP
FWIP
FWIP
I...
KA-CHK

TO SAVE PEOPLE AND BRING SMILES TO AS MANY FACES AS I CAN. THAT IS MY MISSION.

HEALING SHOT!

DWOOOM

INCREDIBLE!

YOU TRULY EARN THE TITLE OF CLERIC! LUNA, Y--

TWIST

WHUMP
LUNA?!
WHUP

......

YIKES...

CHATTER CHATTER CHATTER

TWITCH TWITCH

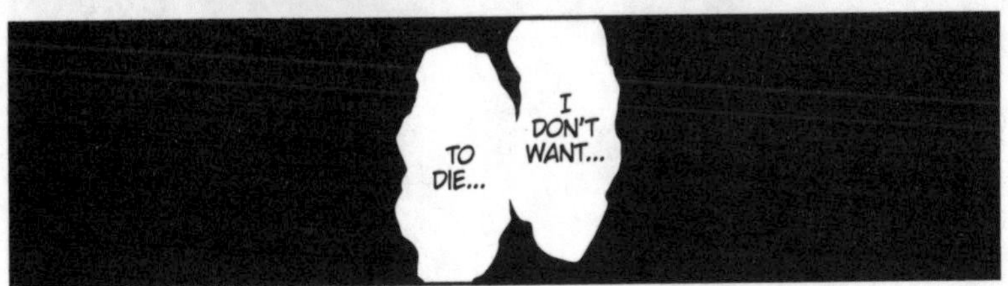

TWITCH

CHATTER
CHATTER
CHATTER

CURSES ...

ARE SCARY ...

TWITCH

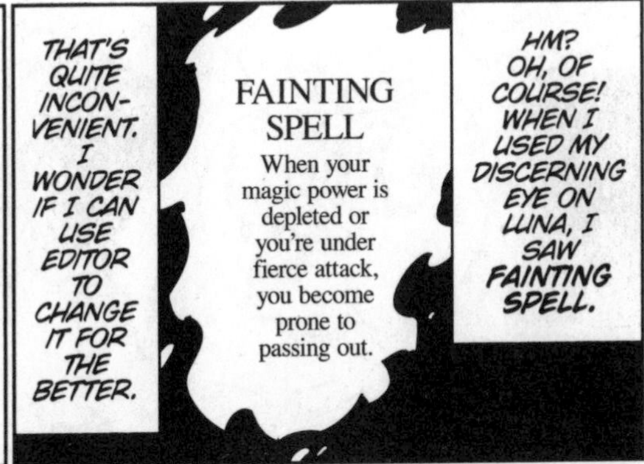
HM? OH, OF COURSE! WHEN I USED MY DISCERNING EYE ON LUNA, I SAW FAINTING SPELL.
FAINTING SPELL
When your magic power is depleted or you're under fierce attack, you become prone to passing out.
THAT'S QUITE INCONVENIENT. I WONDER IF I CAN USE EDITOR TO CHANGE IT FOR THE BETTER.

HUH? WAIT, MAYBE...

THUT
THUT
AW, I KNEW IT!
THUT
THIS ALWAYS HAPPENS TO LUNA.

IT'S ALL RIGHT. SHE'LL WAKE UP SOON.
PAT PAT PAT
URGH...
IT'S TRUE. SHE SEEMS USED TO THIS.
MNF... MAMA ...?
YES, THIS IS MAMA. WAKE UP NOW, SWEETIE!
WHUH...?

TWO MINUTES LATER.
Y-Y-YOU SHOULDN'T HAVE WITNESSED THAT SHAMEFUL SCENE!
PLEASE FORGET WHAT YOU JUST SAW! PLEASE!!
WHICH PART DOES SHE MEAN? ALL OF IT...?

NOW THEN. LET'S GO TO MISS MARIA, WHO REQUIRES OUR AID! COME ALONG!
BOOM
SWEAT SWEAT
BUT...
WHAT? WITH ME ON THE CASE, YOU NEEDN'T WORRY! THERE'S NOTHING TO FEAR!

PAT
SHOULD WE TRY TO THINK OF ANOTHER WAY?
WHAT'S THAT?! ARE YOU SAYING WE SHOULD JUST LEAVE HER TO DIE?!
LUNA, YOUR LEGS...
TH-THEY'RE QUIVERING IN ANTICIPATION!
SHUDDER SHUDDER
SHUDDER
YOU SAID, "CURSES ARE SCARY"!
HUH? YOU WERE LYING?

BAM
IF YOU LIFT THE CURSE, YOU'LL DIE?
THIS IS THE FIRST I'VE HEARD OF THIS, LUNA.
......!

AND WE CALL OURSELVES CLOSE FRIENDS?!

IT MAKES ME SICK!

EEP...

SICK OF MYSELF FOR BEING SO THICK-HEADED!
I'M SORRY...
I'M SORRY I NEVER KNEW WHAT YOU WERE STRUGGLING WITH.

YOU'RE ALWAYS LIKE THIS, LUNA! YOU PUT EVERYONE ELSE FIRST!

YOU CAN LEAN ON ME, YOU KNOW.

LUNA, YOU IDIOT...

THESE
TWO ARE
LOVELY
TOGETHER.

LET'S FIGURE OUT A WAY AROUND USING YOUR LIFT CURSE SKILL.
BUT IF WE DO THAT, THEN ...!
IT'S OKAY.
I'VE COME TO REALIZE THAT THE SITUATION ISN'T HOPELESS.

IN FACT, IT MAY BE CHANGING FOR THE BETTER.

HUH?!

THERE'S STILL A CHANCE TO SAVE MARIA.

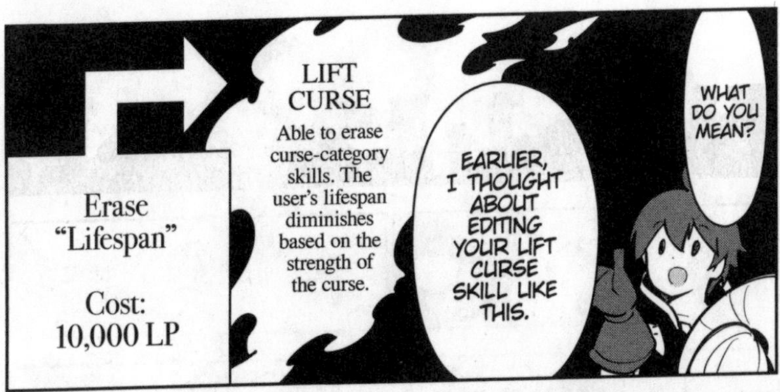
WHAT DO YOU MEAN?
EARLIER, I THOUGHT ABOUT EDITING YOUR LIFT CURSE SKILL LIKE THIS.
LIFT CURSE
Able to erase curse-category skills. The user's lifespan diminishes based on the strength of the curse.
Erase "Lifespan"
Cost: 10,000 LP

THAT'S EXPEN-SIVE...
REMOVING MARIA'S CURSE WOULD BE CHEAPER.
LP Cost
10,000
8,000
MARIA 1
LUNA EDIT 2
SIX OF ONE, HALF A DOZEN OF ANOTHER... MORE OR LESS.
SO THEN, I THOUGHT ABOUT CHANGING IT LIKE THIS...

"The user's lifespan diminishes"
↓
Change to:
"The user's **money** diminishes"
4000 LP
0
1
2
4,000
3
NO WAY! HALF THE PRICE?!

THIS WAY, YOU WON'T HAVE TO SACRIFICE YOURSELF, LUNA.
WE CAN SAVE MARIA...
AND I'LL ONLY HAVE TO ACQUIRE HALF AS MUCH LP.

WE CAN ACCOMPLISH OUR GOAL WITHOUT A SINGLE PERSON HAVING TO SUFFER.

THAT'S WONDERFUL! TO THINK WE CAN SETTLE ALL OF THIS!
PLEASE USE EDITOR ON ME!
I WILL. BUT RIGHT NOW...
I DON'T HAVE ENOUGH LP TO DO THE EDIT.

I NEED ABOUT 2000 MORE LP.
Because if I get down to 0 LP, I'll die.
5000
2000 LP
More
INSURANCE
2400 LP
Current
+500 LP
2500
WHEN I GET PHYSICAL WITH THE OPPOSITE SEX, EAT GOURMET FOOD, OR FEEL SATISFACTION FROM ACHIEVING A GOAL, I EARN A LOT OF LP.
OHH!

IS THERE ANY WAY I CAN GET IT ALL AT ONCE?
YES! THERE'S AN EVENT THAT'S PERFECT FOR THOSE CONDITIONS.
A NOBLE-MAN HOLDS IT EVERY WEEK.
OH!

AND IT'S CALLED...
WHPP
IT'S CALLED ...?!

RRRRRMMMBB

YOU'VE WAITED LONG ENOUGH, YOU SWINE!
GLEEEEEAM

WE HAVE AGAIN GATHERED TEN ENVIABLE--YET FOOLHARDY--MEN.
CHATTER
CHATTER
THESE OUTRAGEOUS FELLOWS WILL BRAG ABOUT THEIR WOMEN AND TRY TO WIN THE ONE MILLION REL PRIZE!

WE NOW OPEN THE HAREM PRIDE EVENT!!
オRR
オ
オAA
オAA
オAA
オHH
オ
オHH
TODAY, ONCE AGAIN, IT'S TIME TO VENT YOUR STRESS ON THESE SMUG NORMIES!
HUFF HUFF
HAAAH HAAAH

THE HOST WAS BETRAYED BY WOMEN SEVERAL TIMES IN THE PAST.

AND ALL THE MEN GATHERED HERE...

HAD SIMILAR EXPERIENCES.

APPARENTLY, THE MAJORITY OF THEM DON'T HAVE SWEETHEARTS.

DEFEAT THESE LADIES' MEN! WRECK THEIR HAREMS!

Chapter 11 / End

THE
HIDDEN
DUNGEON
ONLY I CAN
ENTER

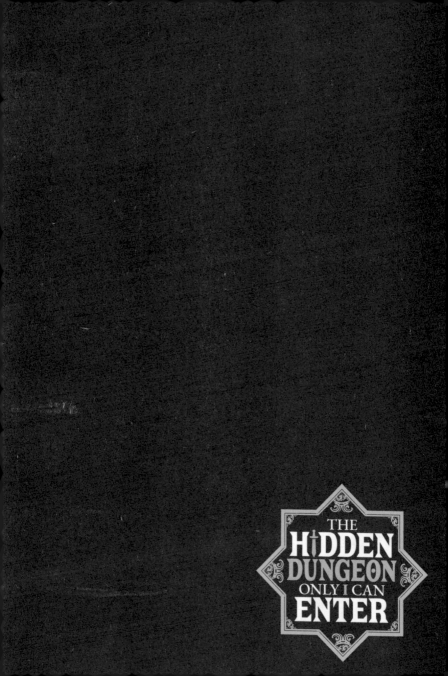

Chapter 12: Insult Tournament

Maria's Residence
Duke Albert Manor

HAHH!
HAHH!
WE'VE DONE ALL WE CAN.
I'M VERY SORRY.

EVERY-ONE, WE SHOULD SAY OUR GOOD-BYES.

WE'RE OUT OF TIME, NOIR.
WHERE ARE YOU?

HURRY UP AND START!

PREPARE TO BE PUNCHING BAGS! YOU'RE GONNA GET PUMMELED!!

IT WAS THE RIGHT CHOICE TO ENTER THIS TOURNAMENT...

TO GET THE LP I NEED TO SAVE MARIA.

EMMA HAS BEEN A FRIEND SINCE WE WERE LITTLE.
SHE UNDER-STANDS ME BETTER THAN ANYONE.

LOLA IS A RELIABLE BUSINESS PARTNER.
SHE HAS A DEEPLY KIND AND FRIENDLY HEART.

LUNA IS A YOUNG CLERIC WHO HAS FOUND HER CALLING IN LIFE.
I HAVE FAITH IN THEM. THERE'S NOTHING TO FEAR!

ENTRY NUMBER ONE!
HAREM PERSONNEL, STEP FORWARD, ONE AT A TIME!

HELLO, I'M MIRA! I WORK IN A RESTAURANT! ♪
SMOOCH
GRIN

HUSSSH
GRUMBLE
FEEL LIKE...
HUH ...?

FEEL LIKE I'M GONNA PUKE! BLARRGH!

PLEASE DO SOMETHING ABOUT THAT PIG SNOUT!

YOU FUGLY TURD! WHY DON'T YOU GET REINCARNATED IN ANOTHER WORLD TO FIX YOURSELF?!

THE ONLY GOOD THING IS YER HAIR! THE REST OF YA'S SO FOUL IT'S HILARIOUS. YOU EVEN MAKE FOOD TASTE BAD!

THIS WILL BE A BRUTAL BATTLE.
FWM
FWM

DASH
ENOUGH ALREADY! THIS IS WHY NOT A SINGLE ONE OF YOU HAS A GIRL-FRIEND!
WHO NEEDS 'EM?!
IF YOU'RE GONNA WALK AROUND WITH THAT HAG...
MIGHT AS WELL GET A DOG!

GO HOME! ♪
GO HOME! ♪
THE SPEC-TATORS CAME HERE TO HURL ABUSE.
SO THE OTHER WOMEN ENTRY NUMBER ONE BROUGHT ARE ALSO BEING BULLIED.
GO HOME! ♪

NOW, WAIT!
STOP!
THEY ONLY GET TO LEAVE ONCE I'VE GIVEN THEM SCORES. HERE I GO!

STARTING FROM THE RIGHT, OUT OF A MAXIMUM POSSIBLE SCORE OF 1000 POINTS EACH... 30 POINTS, 26 POINTS, AND 20 POINTS.
CRAK
THAT'S A TOTAL OF 76 POINTS OUT OF 3000!
HUH? ISN'T THAT, LIKE, WAY LOW?

EXIT
THIS PLACE IS MORE BRUTAL THAN A DUNGEON.

URGH...
I REALLY WANNA GO HOME...

NO PROBLEM. GO AHEAD.
NOIR'S GOT ME, AT LEAST.

I'M NOT LEAVING! I CAN STAND UP TO THOSE INSULTS!
CHOOM
WELL PLAYED, LOLA! SHE REVIVED EMMA JUST LIKE THAT!

THE NEXT TEAMS TO TAKE THE STAGE FACED STORMS OF ABUSE, TOO, EXCEPT FOR...
760 POINTS!
HMM. BEAUTIFUL...
THE HOST IS A NOBLEMAN. IF HE ACCEPTS THAT SOMEONE IS BEAUTIFUL, HE DOES SEEM TO GIVE THEM A DECENT SCORE.

AND THEN CAME THE UPSET OF ENTRY NUMBER NINE.

THEM?!

WHAT'S WRONG?

WHOA! A BEVY OF EXCEPTIONAL BEAUTIES!

THEY'RE A TEAM OF ADVEN-TURERS FROM A RIVAL GUILD, LAHMU.

THEY GOT AROUND 900 POINTS EACH, FOR AN INCREDIBLE 2700 POINTS TOTAL!

THIS IS NO TIME TO BE ADMIRING THEM. WE NEED TO *BEAT* THEM!

CAN'T STOP SHAKING. I MEAN...
ブース
UGLY!
ブース
HOMELY!
IT'S POSSIBLE I'LL HAVE TO WATCH THEM GET BULLIED RIGHT IN FRONT OF ME.

CLATTER RATTLE
HURRY UP AND SHOW US WHATCHA GOT!
OH NO. SHE'S TOO NERVOUS.
HOOH
SHUDDER
WHAH?! ♡

BOING
BOING
GOOD. SHE'S NOT SO STIFF NOW.
AND SHE'S GOT SOME BOUNCE IN HER STEP.
SHE REALLY IS BOUNCING LIKE CRAZY...!
HRRMM...

M-MY NAME IS EMMA. I'VE STARTED ATTENDING THE HERO ACADEMY.
UMM...
I'M LIKE A NEWBORN CHICKADEE STILL...SO I MIGHT NOT ALWAYS BE HELPFUL...
BUT ONE THING I CAN DO IS STAY BY YOUR SIDE AND LISTEN TO YOUR WORRIES.

PLEASE, FEEL FREE TO SPEAK YOUR MINDS!
IF I COULD BURY ...

IF I COULD BURY MY FACE IN THAT CHEST, MY TROUBLES WOULD JUST...FLY AWAY.
GLOOM
WHAT'S MORE, SHE ATTENDS THE HERO ACADEMY. THAT'S ELITE! AND SHE ALSO HAS A NICE PERSONALITY.

PHEW!
THANK GOODNESS. THEY DIDN'T BADMOUTH HER.

I'M LUNA. I'M A CLERIC AND AN ADVENTURER.

IF ANY OF YOU ARE HURT, PLEASE LET ME KNOW.

I'LL BLAST HEALING AT YOU WITH MY MAGIC PISTOLS!

ISN'T THAT *THE* LUNA?! *URK*...! I DIDN'T KNOW SHE HAD A MAN!

GLOOM

COULD YOU HEAL MY BITTER HEART?

I'M LOLA! I'M A RECEPTIONIST AT ODIN!

YOU COULD BE A FUTURE ADVENTURER! PLEASE COME SEE US SOON!

WE SEEM TO HAVE EARNED THE HOST'S RECOGNITION, TOO. EACH OF THE GIRLS GOT OVER 950 POINTS...

FOR A TOTAL OF ABOUT 2900 POINTS, MEANING...

HOORAY! WE WON!!

NOT SO FAST!
GLEEEAM
HUH ...?

I FORGOT TO MENTION, YOU ONLY WIN AFTER EVERYONE IN THE ARENA AGREES TO IT.
SAY WHAT? THAT'S NO FAIR!
SILENCE! I MAKE THE RULES HERE!

SO, NOW COMES THE REAL TEST, HUH?
HFF!
HFF!
THE HAREM MEMBERS WILL DEMONSTRATE THEIR LOVE FOR THEIR MASTER ACCORDING TO THE SCENARIOS I DICTATE.

THERE ARE THREE.
WHAM
① Your master is shivering on a cold night. What do you do?
② What do you do when your master catches a cold?
③ Prove that yours is the ultimate harem!
THEY'RE SO SPECIFIC!

ARE YOU COLD? WE'LL WARM YOU UP RIGHT NOW!

YES, THAT'S GOOD. YOU'RE NOT COLD ANYMORE, ARE YOU?!

OOH! IT'S LIKE THEY'RE COMFORT-ING A CHILD...

HUH?! WHAT THE HECK ?!!

NUZZLE

THEY'RE SNUG-GLING UP TO HIM TO GENE-RATE WARMTH?!

NUZZLE

WHAT DO YOU DO WHEN YOUR MASTER CATCHES A COLD?
USE THIS PROP, TOO!
POFF
YOU ALWAYS WORK SO HARD!

YOU SHOULD REST WHEN YOU HAVE A COLD, OKAY?
RUB
RUB
PAT
PAT
HURRN...

......
CRNCH

HEE HEE! NOIR! SAY, "AH"! ♡
FOR REALS?
BUT THAT'S COLD BREAD! IT'S NOT WARM AT ALL!

HER BEHAVIOR IS SO NATURAL... AS IF SHE'D ALWAYS GIVE YOU FRESHLY BAKED BREAD!!
AHH!
DELISH!
じゅっ…
WAAAAAAA
WHAT THE...? THIS ISN'T WHAT IT'S LIKE FOR ME WHEN I HAVE A COLD...
WHAT'S WITH THESE PEOPLE ?!

LONG AGO...MY OWN WIFE AND DAUGHTER ALSO... URK! NEXT!
HEEH!
HEEH!
THE FINAL HAREM DISPLAY! COME ON!

THE LAST THING IS TO PROVE THAT WE'RE THE ULTIMATE HAREM.
WHAT DO THEY PLAN TO DO?

CHFF

READY, SET...

OOOOOCH
ゅぱっ

SM

MY EYES ARE SWEATING...

WAAAAHH!

GUSSSH

GYAA-AAHH! NO! STOP ALREADY!

I CAN SEE THE FACES OF MY WIFE AND DAUGHTER!

DON'T MAKE ME REMEMBER A PAST THAT I CAN NEVER HAVE BAAACK!

WHUMP
TWITCH
TWITCH
UMM...
SO THEN, WHAT'S THE VERDICT?

THWUMP
THAT'S THE PRIZE MONEY...

YOU'VE ALREADY WON...
SO GET OUT OF MY SIGHT!
BWAAAH!
WAAHH!

AND THAT'S HOW WE WON A MILLION RELS.
IT WAS ALL THANKS TO EMMA AND THE OTHERS.

THEIR ROLE-PLAYING, AND THE SATISFACTION I GOT FROM WINNING THE TOURNAMENT, BROUGHT MY LP UP TO...
4900! TARGET ACHIEVED!

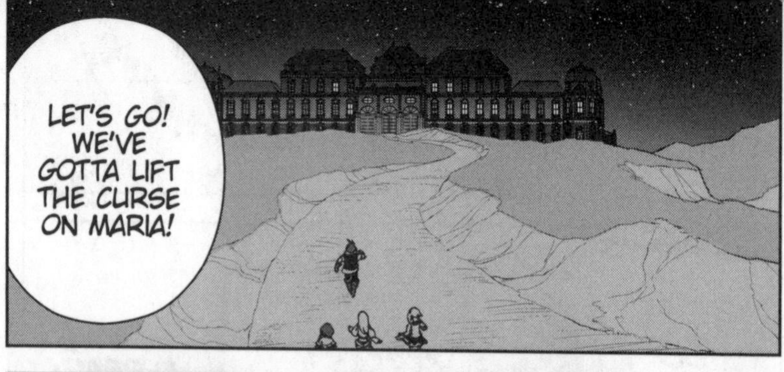

LET'S GO! WE'VE GOTTA LIFT THE CURSE ON MARIA!

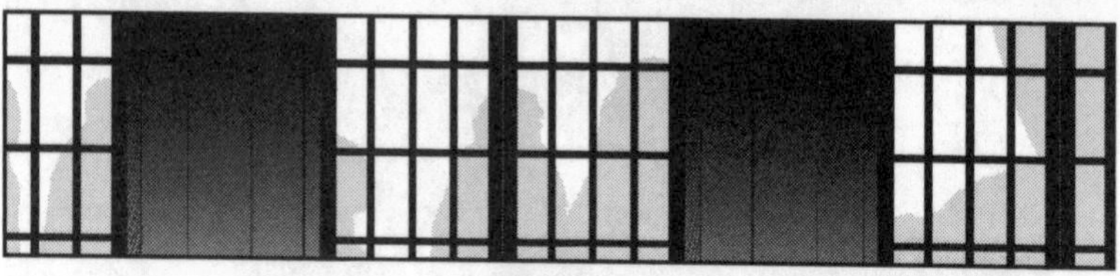

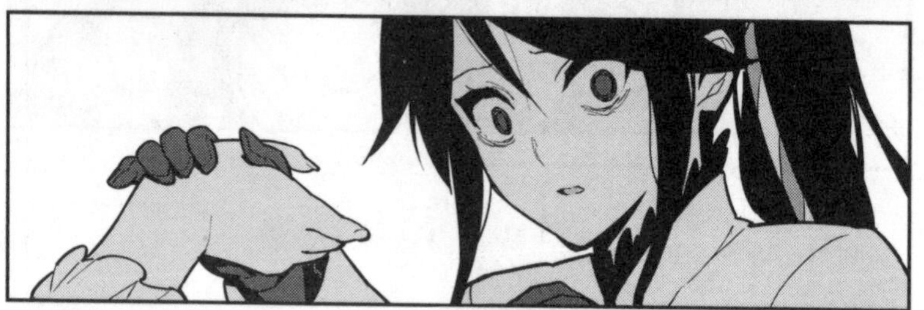

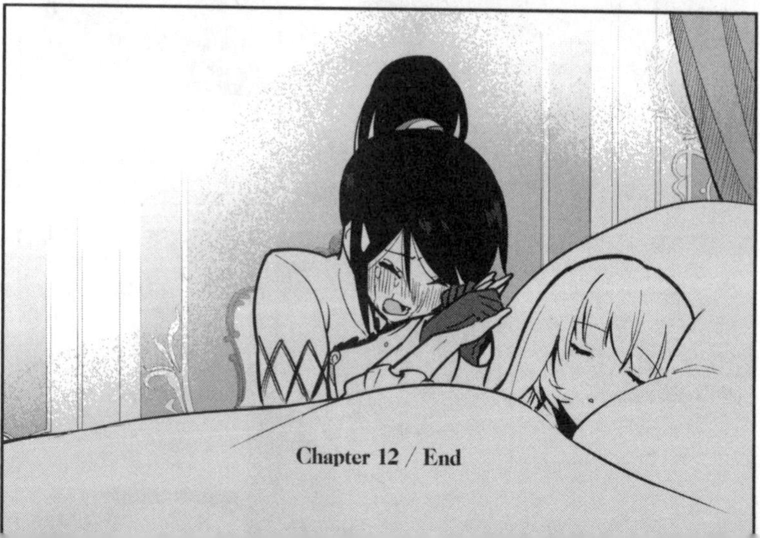

Chapter 12 / End

◆ I WISH I COULD SMELL THE FRAGRANCE OF BIG BROTHER'S HAIR ALL DAY LONG ◆

THE
HIDDEN
DUNGEON
ONLY I CAN
ENTER

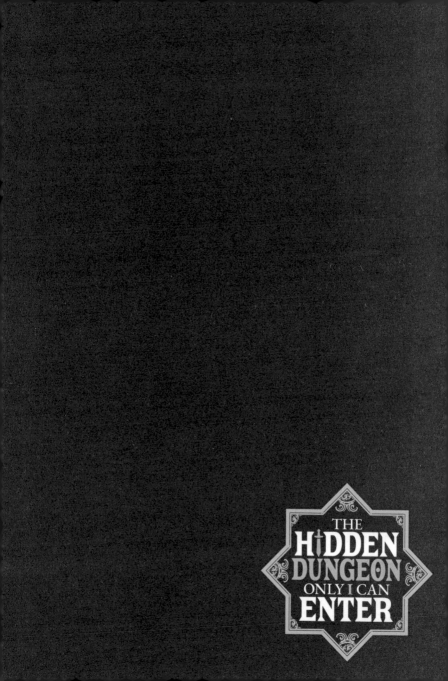

Chapter 13: The Curse

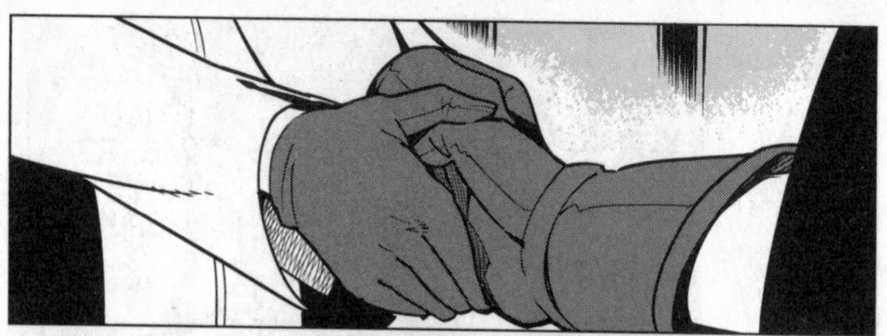

I'M SO SORRY, AMANE. I USED ONE OF MY SKILLS TO SNEAK A PEEK AT MARIA'S INFORMATION.
I KNOW ABOUT HER CURSE.
BUT THAT'S ALSO WHY I KNOW...

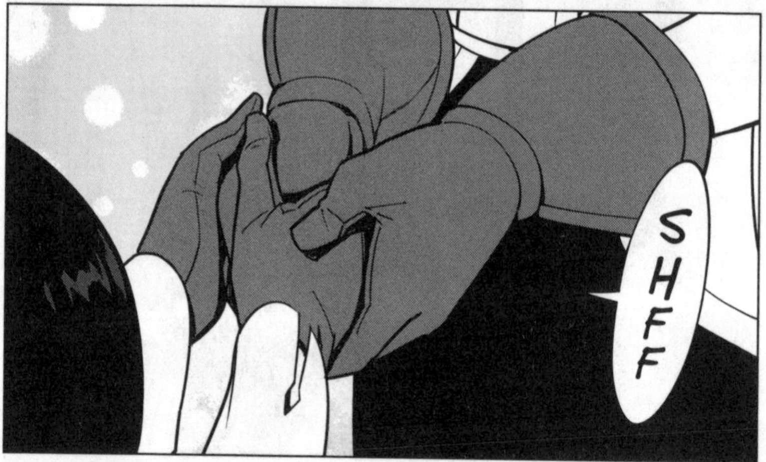
SHFF

THAT THERE'S STILL TIME TO SAVE HER!

AFTER ALL, IT'S NOT HER SIXTEENTH BIRTHDAY YET.

TICK

TICK

TICK

TICK

TICK

TICK

TICK

FOR AS LONG AS I CAN REMEMBER, I'VE UNDERSTOOD...

THAT I'M FATED TO DIE WITHOUT EVER BECOMING AN ADULT.

DEAR GOD... WHY HAVE YOU DONE SUCH A CRUEL THING TO ME?

THE CHURCH USED DISCERNING EYE ON ME, AND THEY DISCOVERED THAT I HAD THE SIXTEENTH YEAR DEATH CURSE.
WE LET THE WORLD THINK I HAD A WEAK CONSTITUTION, AND KEPT THE TRUTH OF THE CURSE SECRET.

IT'S HARD TO ENDURE THE PAINS THAT SEIZE MY ENTIRE BODY.
IF I DIDN'T HAVE MY FAMILY AND AMANE TO SUPPORT ME...
I PROBABLY WOULD HAVE BEEN GONE FROM THIS WORLD BY NOW.

A SORCERER CAST THIS CURSE ON ONE OF MY ANCESTORS TWO HUNDRED YEARS AGO, AFTER BEING DEFEATED BY HIM.

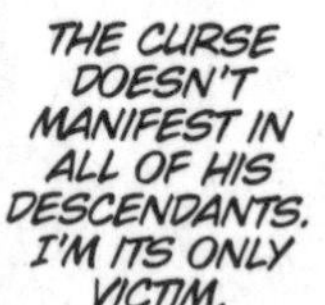
THE CURSE DOESN'T MANIFEST IN ALL OF HIS DESCENDANTS. I'M ITS ONLY VICTIM.

EVEN THE COMBINED POWER OF THE FOREMOST CURSE BREAKERS COULD NOT LIFT IT. THEY'RE AT THEIR WITS' END.
DEAR GOD, I WILL SUFFER THE CURSE IN MARIA'S PLACE IF YOU'LL LET ME...
FATHER, NO! IF ANYONE, I SHOULD TAKE HER PLACE!

KA-TAK
YOU HAVE TO TAKE OVER THE FAMILY, BIG BROTHER. I'M YOUNGER. I SHOULD TAKE ON THE CURSE.
IT'S SO STRANGE. I WAS BORN WITH THE WORST OF MIS-FORTUNES, BUT RIGHT NOW...

I'M FILLED WITH A WARMTH LIKE NO OTHER.

WHAT? YOU WANT TO TAKE THE EXAM FOR THE HERO ACADEMY?

YES.
EVERYONE TREATED MY FEELINGS WITH RESPECT.
OF COURSE, I WILL TAKE THE EXAM ALONG WITH MARIA.
AND WE'RE BOTH SURE TO PASS. YOU'LL SEE.

IF I COULDN'T ESCAPE THE SIXTEENTH YEAR DEATH CURSE...

THUS RESOLVED, I WAS IN THE MIDDLE OF THE ENTRANCE EXAM, WHEN...

I WITNESSED A CERTAIN PERSON HEAVE A SPECIAL STONE BULLET.
YAGH!

I'D THOUGHT THAT STONE BULLETS ONLY CAME IN A SPECIFIC SIZE.
THAT WAS HUGE!

WHO IS HE ...?
NOIR STARDIA. HE'S AN EXAMINEE, LIKE US.
IT'S POSSIBLE THAT HE POSSESSES THE EDITOR SKILL.
THE LEGENDARY ADVENTURER OLIVIA'S SPECIAL SKILL?

YOU SAW IT, TOO, DIDN'T YOU, AMANE? THE SIZE OF THAT STONE BULLET CAN'T BE EXPLAINED BY ANYTHING OTHER THAN EDITOR.
THAT IS TRUE...
ONE DAY, I'D LIKE TO ASK NOIR IF HE HAS THE EDITOR SKILL, AND IF HE COULD USE IT ON MY CURSE...

IT CAN'T BE... NOIR ...?!

WHY IS HE HERE? COULD AMANE HAVE CALLED HIM...?

NOIR SEEMS TO BE EXPLAINING ABOUT HIS OWN ABILITIES, DISCERNING EYE, AND LP.

WHAT'S MORE, LUNA HAS GIVEN HER TRUE REASON FOR REFUSING TO LIFT MY CURSE BEFORE.
YOU HAVE TO PAY WITH YOUR OWN LIFESPAN?!
BUT THEN... YOU'LL ...!

IT'S ALL RIGHT. I USED MY EDITOR SKILL TO CHANGE THE COST OF LUNA'S SKILL FROM LIFESPAN TO MONEY.
SO, YOU DO HAVE THE EDITOR SKILL.
MARIA GUESSED RIGHT.
HUH?!

SHE FIGURED IT OUT? SHE HAS SHARP POWERS OF OBSER-VATION, HUH?
......
NATURALLY. SHE NEVER TOOK HER EYES OFF YOU.

HUH?!

THE TRUTH IS...
MARIA HAS ALWAYS BEEN PASSIVE AND AWKWARD WITH MEN.
BUT LATELY, ALL SHE TALKS ABOUT IS YOU, NOIR.
MAYBE THAT'S WHY...
SHE'S BECOME SO CHEERFUL. SHE'S LIKE A WHOLE NEW PERSON, AND SHE'S OVERCOME HER FEAR OF MEN.
AMANE... WHAT ARE YOU DOING?!
WHY ARE YOU BLABBING ABOUT ALL OF THIS?!
I'M NOT EVEN ASLEEP!

MARIA HAS CHANGED SINCE SHE MET YOU, NOIR.

THANK YOU.
SHE WAS REBORN BECAUSE OF YOU.

AMANE... I TOLD YOU THOSE THINGS IN SECRET.
JOLT
M-MARIA?! HOW LONG HAVE YOU BEEN AWAKE...?!

NOIR...
WHY HAVE YOU...

WHY HAVE YOU DONE ALL THIS FOR ME?
I... HAVE NOTHING TO OFFER YOU.

OH NO! DON'T TELL ME YOU'VE FORGOTTEN.
SHFF
!

"NOIR.
"WOULD YOU PLEASE JOIN HANDS WITH ME?"
YOU ACKNOWLEDGED ME THAT TIME.
YOU'VE GIVEN ME PLENTY.
SO MUCH THAT MY HEART'S OVERFLOWING.

I'VE JUST EDITED LUNA'S LIFT CURSE, SO I'M A LITTLE BIT DIZZY.
A STEADY SUPPLY OF LP IS ESSENTIAL TO ACTIVATE MY SKILLS.
AND I CAN ACQUIRE LP BASED ON MY DEGREE OF HAPPINESS, SO...
STARE

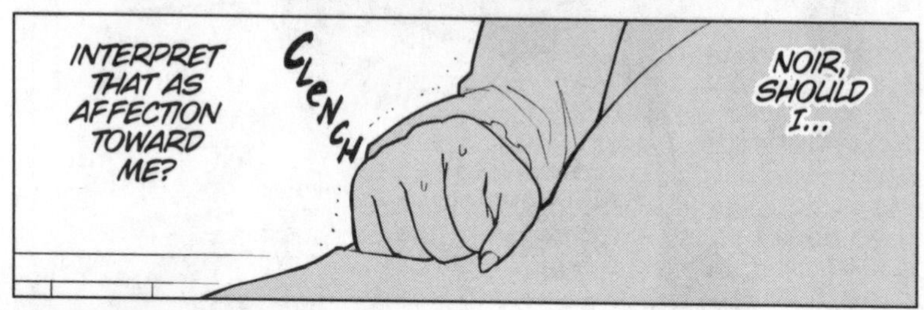
NOIR, SHOULD I...
CLENCH
INTERPRET THAT AS AFFECTION TOWARD ME?

......
AH...! DEAR GOD.
YOU REALLY ARE BEING CRUEL TO ME.
BA-DUMP
IF ALL YOU'D GIVEN ME WAS A LIFE OF SUFFER-ING...
GRIP
HUH? MARI--
I COULD HAVE DIED WITHOUT ANY REGRETS.
BA-DUMP
BUT NOW, OF ALL TIMES...
BA-DUMP
YOU GRANT ME A LIFE OF HAPPI-NESS.
BA-DUMP

I GOT TO MEET YOU...
THANKS TO THIS CURSE.
BA-DUMP

BA-DUMP
AND NOW YOU'RE...
THE ONLY THING I SEE ANY-MORE.

......

I WILL LIFT THE CURSE NOW.
CLOSE YOUR EYES.

BA-DUMP
BA-DUMP

BA-
DUMP
TICK

BA-
DUMP
TICK

BA-
DUMP
TWAAAAAAAHH
TICK

Chapter 13 / End

BIG BROTHER, WHERE COULD YOU BE SO LATE AT NIGHT?
I HOPE YOU HAVEN'T BEEN IN AN ACCI-DENT.
I AM YOUR SISTER OF FINE CHARAC-TER, AND I CAN'T SLEEP FOR WORRY.

PING
MY RADAR'S GOING OFF...
THAT WOMAN'S LOVE PRES-SURE IS BECOMING HEIGHT-ENED?
THAT WOMAN WHO'S ALWAYS AROUND BIG BROTHER...
LOVE PRESSURE
Romantic energy that closes in around Noir.
KEH HEH HEH
AND THERE'RE THREE--NO, FOUR OF THEM?!
GEH HEH HEH
THE LOVE PRES-SURE IS... INCREAS-ING...?

BIG BROTHER, WHERE COULD YOU BE SO LATE AT NIGHT?
I'M SO VERY WORRIED ABOUT YOU.

THE
HIDDEN
DUNGEON
ONLY I CAN
ENTER

Chapter 14:
Apprentice

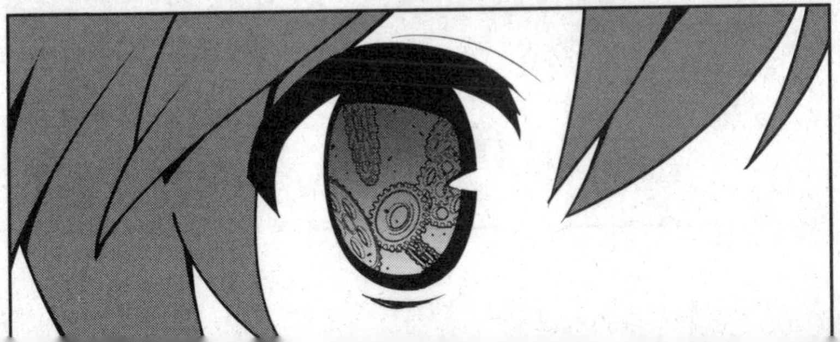

THE PAIN IN MY CHEST... HAS VANISHED.
IT'S LIKE IT WAS ALL A DREAM.
I CHECKED WITH MY DISCERNING EYE, TOO.

THE SIXTEENTH YEAR DEATH CURSE IS COMPLETELY GONE.

YOUR FAMILY'S ANGUISH IS OVER NOW, TOO.
IT'S ALL RIGHT.
SHFF
NO ONE NEEDS TO SUFFER ANY-MORE.

TH...
THANK YOU...
THE FOG HAS FINALLY BEEN LIFTED FROM MY HEART AS WELL.

I CAN'T SAY HOW GRATEFUL I AM.

I'LL BE REPAYING THIS DEBT FOR THE REST OF MY LIFE.

TH-THERE'S NO NEED TO EXAG-GERATE...

ISN'T THIS GREAT, MARIA?
YES.
YES, IT TRULY IS.
YEAH.

SWSH
?

DO YOU THINK MAR... FALLEN FOR HIM?
SHE'S... ALREADY... NOIR... CAPTIVE...
GRRR... YET ANOTHER... RIVAL FOR...

THE TRUTH IS... I'M ALSO... LITTLE BIT...
WHAH?!
WHAT COULD THEY BE TALKING ABOUT? IT'S MAKING ME NERVOUS!

NOIR, YOU SKIRT-CHASING BLOCK-HEAD!
HUH...? WHAT DID I DO WRONG?
THIS ONE TIME, I HAVE TO STRONGLY AGREE WITH EMMA.
IT'S A LADIES-ONLY SECRET. HEH HEH HEH!

SHWFF

ALL I ACCUMULATED THROUGH MY YESTERDAYS...
CLEARED A PATH FOR MARIA'S TOMORROW.
CLENCH
I NEVER IMAGINED THAT BEING USEFUL TO OTHERS COULD FEEL SO INVIGOR-ATING.

THE NEXT DAY. THE HIDDEN DUNGEON.

SO, WE SORTED OUT THE CRISIS. EVERYONE'S SAFE AND SOUND.

HM!♪ AND ALL OF IT THANKS TO THE SKILLS I GRANTED YOU!

I AM, AS ALWAYS, IN YOUR DEBT.

WHAT'S THIS? YOU FEEL A BIT DISTANT.

HMPH!

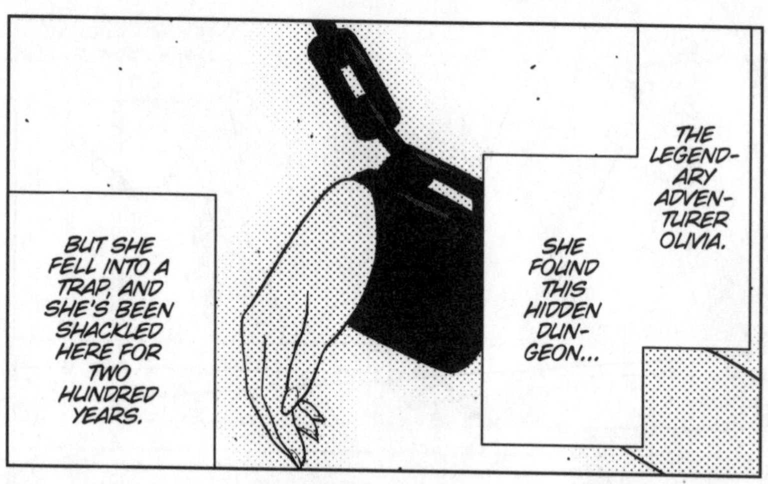
THE LEGENDARY ADVENTURER OLIVIA.
SHE FOUND THIS HIDDEN DUNGEON...
BUT SHE FELL INTO A TRAP, AND SHE'S BEEN SHACKLED HERE FOR TWO HUNDRED YEARS.

ACTUALLY, MASTER...
WHY ARE YOU SO NICE TO ME?

YOU GRANTED ME THAT VALUABLE SKILL SET OUT OF THE BLUE...
AND YOU GIVE ME USEFUL INFORMATION...
WHEN I HAVEN'T REALLY DONE ANYTHING AT ALL.

JOLT
IT'S BECAUSE YOUR SKIN'S SO SMOOTH, NOIR.
IF IT WEREN'T FOR THESE CHAINS, I'D EAT YOU LIKE DESSERT!
A-ALL RIGHT, THEN. GIMME ANOTHER TWO HUNDRED YEARS TO THINK UP A WAY TO GET THOSE CHAINS OFF, OKAY?

"BUT IN TWO HUNDRED YEARS, YOU'LL BE DEAD, NOIR!"
"EH HEH HEH..."
CHFF
CHFF

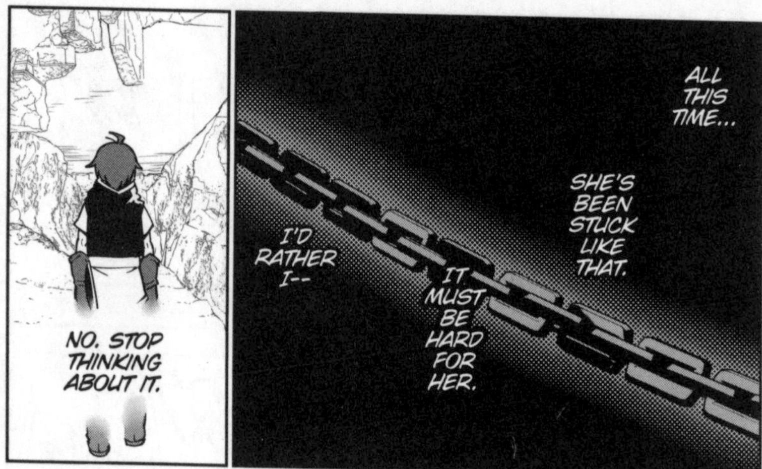
ALL THIS TIME...
SHE'S BEEN STUCK LIKE THAT.
IT MUST BE HARD FOR HER.
I'D RATHER I--
NO. STOP THINKING ABOUT IT.

"WHY ARE YOU SO NICE TO ME?"
......
WHY, I WON-DER?
MAYBE BECAUSE YOUR FACE IS SO SMOOTH, NOIR.

JUST LIKE THAT BOY...

PLEASE, MAKE ME YOUR APPRENTICE!

HUH?

TWO HUNDRED YEARS AGO.

I'M BEG-GING YOU, PLEASE.
グリ QUIVER
グリ QUIVER
AW! HE'S DIRTIED THAT SWEET, SMOOTH FACE.

BUT STILL...
I'M NOT A GOOD TEACHER.
THAT WON'T MATTER! I'LL GIVE IT EVERYTHING I'VE GOT, EVEN IF IT KILLS M--
NO. NEVER. PERIOD.

PUTTING IT TO HIM THAT COLDLY...
HE'S SURE TO GIVE UP.

THE NEXT DAY...
PLEASE, MAKE ME YOUR APPRENTICE!
BOY, WAS I NAIVE!
PLEASE!
PLEASE!
WHY ARE YOU SO OBSESSED...?
BECAUSE I MADE A PROMISE TO MY LATE CHILDHOOD FRIEND THAT I WOULD BECOME THE GREATEST ADVENTURER...
IN THE WORLD.

I WANT TO MAKE MY NAME RESOUND TO THE HEAVENS.
CLENCH
ALL RIGHT, THEN. I'LL GIVE YOU A CHANCE TO BECOME MY APPREN-TICE.
ATTACK ME. RIGHT HERE AND NOW.
HUH...?
NO RULES. IF YOU EVEN SCRATCH ME, YOU WIN.
BUT...RIGHT HERE? IN THE MIDDLE OF TOWN?
YOU WANT TO BE THE WORLD'S GREATEST, DON'T YOU?

HERE I COME!
DASH

VWOOSH
THUT

......!!
YOU'RE THE TYPE THAT CAN'T TELL A LIE, AREN'T YOU?
YOUR SWORD TRAVELS IN FAR TOO STRAIGHT A LINE, AND YOUR EYES LOOK ONLY AT YOUR TARGET.
ANOTHER THING...

THIS MAY BE MEDDLE-SOME OF ME...

BUT YOU SHOULD GIVE UP TRYING TO BECOME AN ADVENTURER.

YOU DIDN'T EVEN MAKE USE OF THIS LOCATION.

MURMUR

MURMUR

YOU COULD'VE SHOUTED, "THIEF!" TO GET STRANGERS TO HELP YOU.

BUT WINNING WITH SUCH AN UNFAIR TACTIC WOULD'VE BEEN--

MURMUR

MURMUR

FINE, THEN. YOU WILL NEVER BE MORE THAN A LOSER IN THE *TRUEST* SENSE OF THE WORD.

THERE ARE FAR MORE CUNNING PEOPLE IN THE WORLD THAN YOU'D THINK.

AND YET, THE BOY NEVER LEARNED HIS LESSON. HE KEPT COMING TO ME.
DAY AFTER DAY AFTER DAY...
PLEASE, TEACH ME ABOUT GOBLINS!
WELL, I SUPPOSE I'M NOT BUSY RIGHT THIS MINUTE... BUT JUST THIS ONCE.
A GOBLIN IS SOMETHING EVEN *YOU* COULD BEAT.
SCRIB SCRIB
BUT IRON GOBLINS YOU NEED TO WATCH OUT FOR. THEIR FLESH IS HARD.
AIM TO STAB THEM IN THE EYES.
I found you! Roar!
I SEE...

ABOUT A MONTH LATER...

SUCH TECHNIQUE...! YOU REALLY ARE EXTRA-ORDINARY, MASTER!

I TOLD YOU, I'M NOT YOUR MASTER!

I DON'T THINK I CAN MIMIC THAT, SO I'LL SWING MY SWORD INSTEAD.

THANK YOU FOR YOUR INVALUABLE ADVICE TODAY!

THUT THUT

THUT THUT

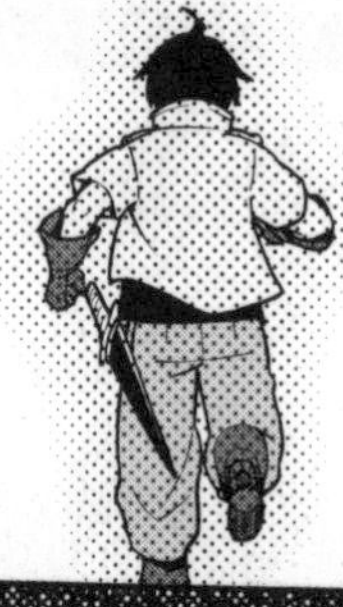

BECAUSE OF YOUR APPREN-TICE.
CLINK
THAT KID ISN'T MY APPREN-TICE.
IS THAT SO? WELL, IF YOU AREN'T ASSOCI-ATES...THEN I SUPPOSE IT DOESN'T MATTER.
PLIP PLIP
WHAT DO YOU MEAN?
WAIT. YOU DON'T KNOW?

A LITTLE WHILE AGO, HE...

CLOP

REVEREND, ARE THESE PEOPLE THIS BOY'S FAMILY?
NO.
APPARENTLY, HE WAS ALONE.
MY DAUGHTER WAS SAVED BY THIS GALLANT LAD.
SWFF

THE DAUGHTER SNUCK PAST THE GUARDS AT THE GATE TO PICK FLOWERS OUTSIDE OF TOWN BY HER-SELF, WHEN...

THE BOY HAPPENED TO BE THERE, AND HE ACTED AS A DECOY SO THAT SHE COULD ESCAPE.

BY THE TIME THE GIRL AND THE GATE GUARDS RAN BACK TO THE SPOT, THE BOY WAS ALREADY...

THOSE WERE THE PARTI-CULARS.
THE BOY WAS SKILLED ENOUGH TO BEAT A GOBLIN, BUT...
HIS ENEMY WAS A RARELY SEEN IRON GOBLIN, A FOR-MIDABLE FOE.
IT WAS TRULY BAD LUCK.
BUT SURPRI-SINGLY...

HIS SWORD WAS BURIED IN THE MONSTER'S EYE.

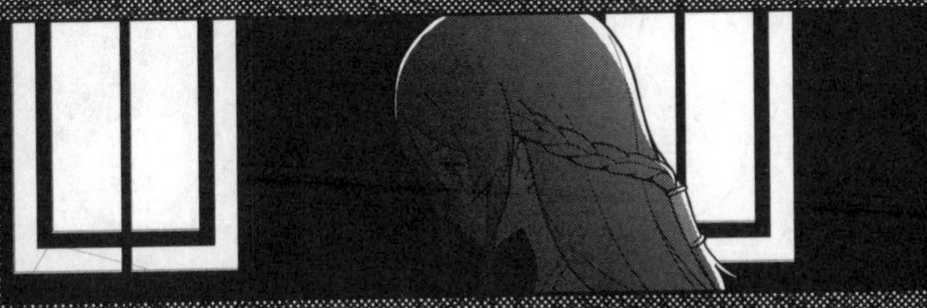

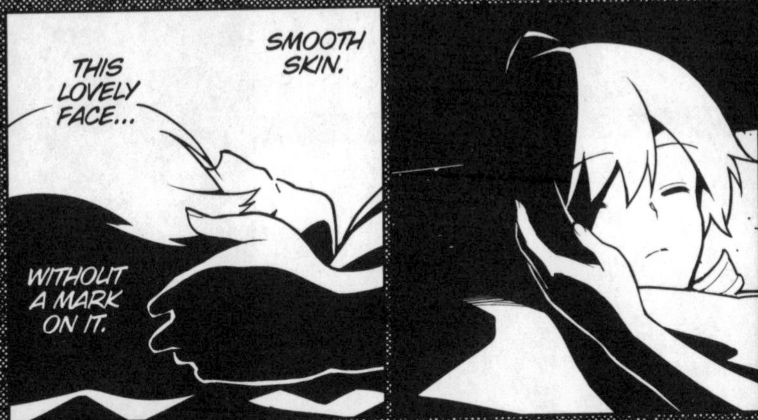

LOVELY.

SUCH A SWEET, TRANQUIL EXPRES- SION...

LIKE THE MOON.

HE REMEMBERED WHAT I'D TOLD HIM.
THAT ENEMY WAS LEVELS ABOVE HIM, BUT HE MANAGED TO BRING IT DOWN.
AND YET...
"PLEASE, MAKE ME YOUR APPRENTICE!"

WHAT IF...
I'D TAUGHT HIM PROPERLY?
WHAT IF...
I'D BECOME HIS MASTER AND GRANTED HIM SKILLS?
IF I'D CHOSEN A DIFFERENT YESTERDAY...
SURELY THERE'D BE A DIFFERENT TOMORROW.

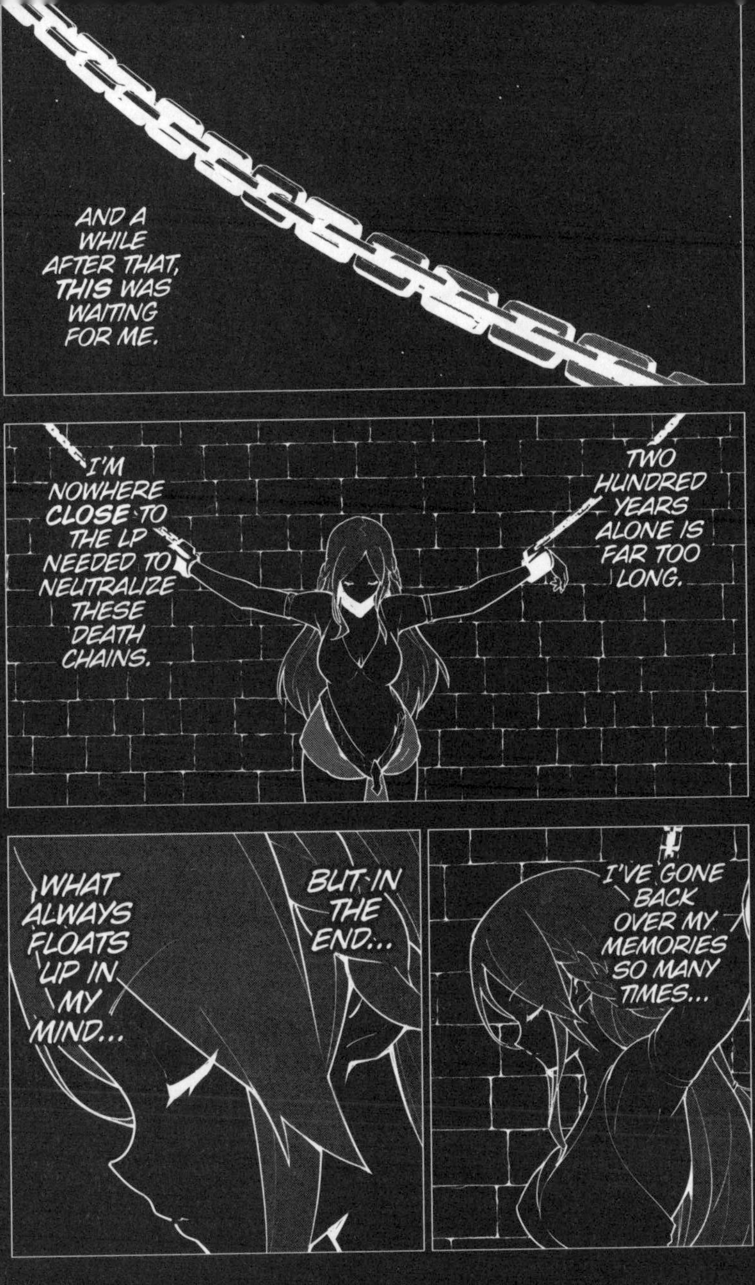

AND A WHILE AFTER THAT, **THIS** WAS WAITING FOR ME.

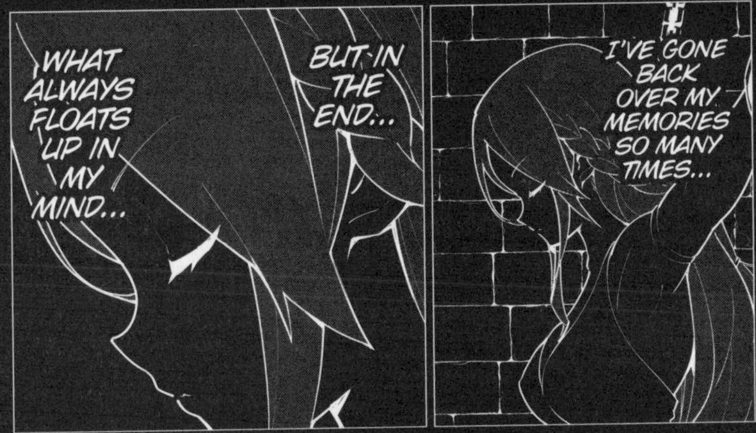

IF I DON'T USE MY TELEPATHY TO REACH THE OUTSIDE WORLD, I'LL GO CRAZY.

"I AWAIT YOU ON THE SECOND FLOOR..."

I'M SURE NO ONE WILL COME...

PLEASE, ANYONE AT ALL, PASS NEARBY...

PLIP

AND THEN, ONE DAY...
DRIP
CHFF

A HUMAN PRES-ENCE! AFTER SO LONG!!
CHFF
I MAY FALL IN LOVE... EVEN IF THEY HAVE THE FACE OF AN ORC.
CHFF
CHFF
CHFF
YOU'RE ALIVE, RIGHT?
......
IS THIS FATE?

I MEAN, YOU'RE JUST SO SIMILAR.
YOU AND THAT BOY.

I GRANTED NOIR MY OWN SKILLS.
EVEN NOW, I CONTINUE TO GIVE HIM MY WISDOM.
HOW SELF-SATISFIED AM I?
MY REGRETS ABOUT THE PAST PROBABLY WON'T GO AWAY.
EVEN SO, I WILL CONTINUE TO POUR INTO NOIR...
EVERY-THING THAT I CAN TEACH HIM.

NOIR, HEY, LISTEN.
WOULD YOU SAY, "MASTER, I'M MAD ABOUT YOU"?
MASTER, I COULD NEVER BE ANGRY WITH YOU.
THAT'S NOT WHAT I MEANT!

NOIR... COME BACK AND SHOW ME HOW YOU'RE DOING.

THAT ALONE WOULD BE ENOUGH...

TO FILL MY HEART WITH WARMTH.

Chapter 14 / End

Extra

I, NOIR STARDIA, AM THE SON OF A FAMILY AT THE VERY BOTTOM RANK OF NOBILITY, AND I WAS LUCKY ENOUGH TO FIND...
NOBILITY
A HIDDEN DUNGEON--A VERY RARE THING IN THE WORLD.
BOY, A LOT SURE HAS HAPPENED!
Password Door
B1F
B2F
B3F
First Battle
Got Skills
Entrance Exam Task
etc...
I'M GOING TO VISIT THE LEGENDARY ADVENTURER, OLIVIA, WHO IS SHACKLED ON THE SECOND FLOOR.

WHOA! NOIR, THAT SMELL!
TODAY, EVEN MORE THAN USUAL...
YOU REEK OF WOMEN.

AH. THAT'S BECAUSE TODAY IS SPECIAL.
OH? HOW SO?

TODAY IS A KISS COMMEM-ORATION DAY.
NOIR... SHALL WE?
BIG BROTH-ER...
IT'S A NORMAL SHOW OF GRATI-TUDE.

THIS IS THANKS FOR REMOVING MY CURSE.
TO OUR FUTURE.
FROM ME, TOO.
DON'T GET THE WRONG IDEA.
IT'S A WEIRD DAY IN WHICH WE EXPRESS OUR APPRECIATION TO THE PEOPLE WHO HAVE HELPED US...WITH A KISS!
WELL, WELL...

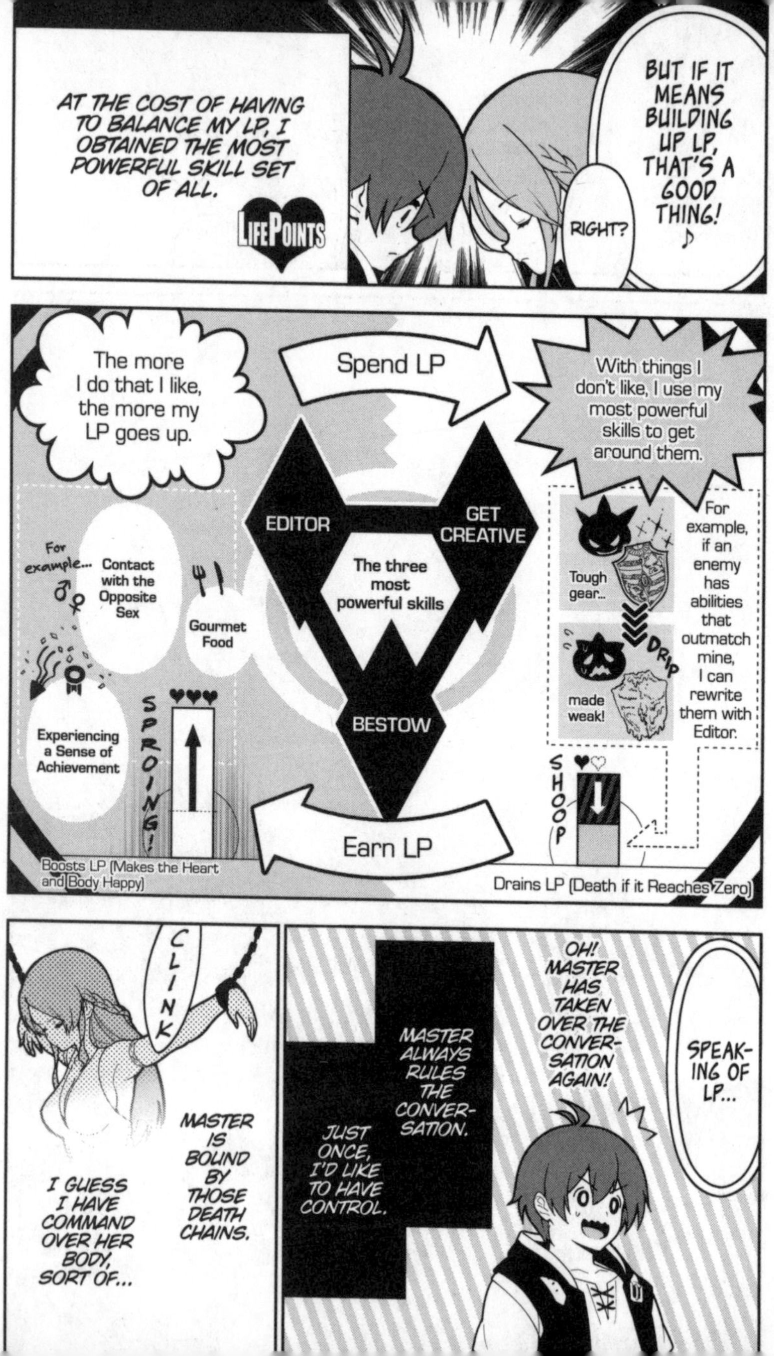

The more I do that I like, the more my LP goes up.

Spend LP

With things I don't like, I use my most powerful skills to get around them.

The three most powerful skills

EDITOR

GET CREATIVE

BESTOW

For example...

Contact with the Opposite Sex

Gourmet Food

Experiencing a Sense of Achievement

SPROING!

Boosts LP (Makes the Heart and Body Happy)

For example, if an enemy has abilities that outmatch mine, I can rewrite them with Editor.

Tough gear...

DRIP

made weak!

SHOOP

Earn LP

Drains LP (Death if it Reaches Zero)

THAT SAID, I REALLY DO LIKE TALKING TO HER.
HA HA HA HA!
MY VOICE BECOMES LIVELIER WHEN WE TALK.
KAH HA HA HA!
SO, WHAT ARE YOU HERE FOR TODAY?
I CAME BECAUSE I WANTED TO TALK TO YOU, MASTER.

ズッキューン
BA DUMP-

I COULD ALMOST CRY... I'M SO GLAD I SURVIVED!
Y-YOU DON'T NEED TO GO THAT FAR!
COME TO THINK OF IT, I DON'T HAVE MANY MEMORIES OF LAUGHING.

AHH...
YOU DON'T SEEM TO HAVE MUCH INTEREST IN OTHER PEOPLE, DO YOU, MASTER?
Human Bonds
Go My way!
YOU'RE RIGHT. I DIDN'T HAVE MANY FRIENDS.
AND SO...

THIS IS THE FIRST TIME I'VE EVER THOUGHT ABOUT SOMEONE LIKE THIS.

NOIR...

PER-HAPS...

......
DOES "SOME-ONE" MEAN ME?
HA HA HA HA!
QUIT WITH THE WEIRD JOKES ALREADY!
HUSSSH
MASTER ...?

I DON'T REALLY UNDER-STAND...
BUT THERE IS ONE THING I KNOW.

ぶっすぅっ
POUT
IT SEEMS I SAID SOMETHING THAT MADE HER SULK...
DO IT.
HUH?

DO IT.
KISS ME.

TODAY IS YOUR KISS COMMEMO-RATION DAY, RIGHT?
WHAAH?!
IT'S NOT FAIR IF I, OLIVIA, AM THE ONLY ONE WHO DOESN'T GET TO KISS YOU.

NO, NO, NO!
I MEAN, THOSE KISSES... I WAS MOSTLY ON THE RECEIVING END.
BA-DUMP
BA-DUMP
GIVING A KISS... WELL, I'M NOT...
VERY EXPERI-ENCED, I GUESS.

I CAN'T DO IT.
IT'S NOT THAT I WOULDN'T.
I'M IMMOBI-LIZED.
BA-DUMP
!
SO, YOU SEE?
YOU HAVE TO DO IT, NOIR.
BA-DUMP

SHFF
BA-DUMP
BA-DUMP
BA-DUMP

BA-DUMP
GULP
BA-DUMP
BA-DUMP

SMOOCH

ぶ〜っ
BOOOOO!
TCH! THAT WAS A CHILD'S KISS!
I'LL LOOK FORWARD TO THE NEXT TIME...
TO AN ADULT KISS THAT WILL SATISFY ME.

BE SURE TO PRAC-TICE WITH LOTS OF DIFFERENT GIRLS!
Y-YES, MA'AM...
I NEVER DID SEIZE CONTROL OF THE CONVER-SATION.
AND I LOST CONTROL OVER MY OWN BODY TO BOOT.
I YIELDED COM-PLETELY.

Extra / End

The Hidden Dungeon
Only I Can Enter

SEVEN SEAS ENTERTAINMENT PRESENTS

THE HIDDEN DUNGEON ONLY I CAN ENTER VOL. 2

story by MEGURU SETO art by TOMOYUKI HINO character design by TAKEHANA NOTE

TRANSLATION
Kumar Sivasubramanian

LETTERING AND RETOUCH
Rai Enril

COVER DESIGN
Nicky Lim

LOGO DESIGN
Arbash

INTERIOR LAYOUT
Christa Miesner

PROOFREADER
Kat Adler
Dawn Davis

EDITOR
Peter Adrian Behravesh

PREPRESS TECHNICIAN
Rhiannon Rasmussen-Silverstein

MANAGING EDITOR
Julie Davis

ASSOCIATE PUBLISHER
Adam Arnold

PUBLISHER
Jason DeAngelis

THE HIDDEN DUNGEON ONLY I CAN ENTER VOL. 2

First published in Japan in 2019 by Kodansha Ltd., Tokyo.
Publication rights for this English edition arranged through Kodansha Ltd., Tokyo.

Seven Seas press and purchase enquiries can be sent to Marketing Manager Lianne Sentar at press@gomanga.com. Information regarding the distribution and purchase of digital editions is available from Digital Manager CK Russell at digital@gomanga.com.

ISBN: 978-1-64827-111-3

Printed in Canada

First Printing: January 2021

10 9 8 7 6 5 4 3 2 1

FOLLOW US ONLINE: ***www.sevenseasentertainment.com***

READING DIRECTIONS

This book reads from ***right to left***, Japanese style. If this is your first time reading manga, you start reading from the top right panel on each page and take it from there. If you get lost, just follow the numbered diagram here. It may seem backwards at first, but you'll get the hang of it! Have fun!!

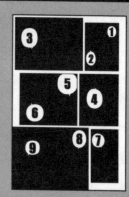

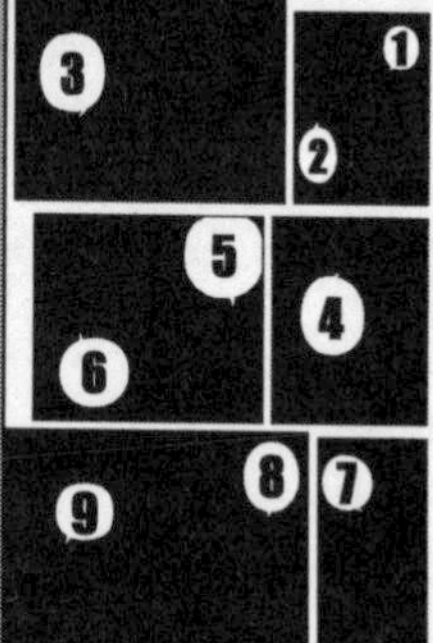